William T. Quick, a native of Indiana, is a full-time writer who lives in a rambling Victorian flat on Russian Hill in San Francisco, California. He is the author of ten published novels, including the seminal cyberpunk cult hit *Dreams of Flesh and Sand*, and the recent prehistoric thriller *The Mammoth Stone*, as well as dozens of shorter works of fiction. He works from home in what is jokingly called his 'legendary' office, where he raises tropical fish and dust bunnies. His friends, both of them, call him Bill. You can visit Bill on the World Wide Web at: "http://www.slip.net/~iceberg/quick.htm".

D1150123

AMERICAN GOTHIC: FAMILY

A novel by W. T. Quick
Based on the Universal Television Series
Created by Shaun Cassidy

CORGI BOOKS

AMERICAN GOTHIC: FAMILY
A CORGI BOOK : 0 552 14541 6

First publication in Great Britain

PRINTING HISTORY
Corgi edition published 1996

A novel by W. T. Quick based on the Universal Television series
created by Shaun Cassidy.

Set in 11/13.5pt Palatino by
Phoenix Typesetting, Ilkley, West Yorkshire.

Corgi Books are published by Transworld Publishers Ltd,
61–63 Uxbridge Road, London W5 5SA,
in Australia by Transworld Publishers (Australia) Pty Ltd,
15–25 Helles Avenue, Moorebank, NSW 2170
and in New Zealand by Transworld Publishers (NZ) Ltd,
3 William Pickering Drive, Albany, Auckland.

Reproduced, printed and bound in Great Britain by
Cox & Wyman Ltd, Reading, Berks.

AMERICAN GOTHIC: FAMILY

Chapter One

In the thundery golden light of that Trinity summer evening, perfect happiness touched Melanie Temple's life for the very last time. Of course, just then, she didn't understand what it was.

So few ever do, and such moments pass unremarked until, days, months, or even years later one looks back with a kind of wonder and says, 'Yes. I remember that . . .'

Some never look back at all.

Melanie Temple, wife of Gage and mother of five-year-old Merlyn, a good woman whose roots thrust deep into the murky tangle of Trinity history and genealogy, sat in her rocking chair before the fire and counted her blessings. The fire crackled peaceably to itself, spitting the odd spark or two, in a reassuring counterpoint to the rhythmic creakings of the old chair on the polished maple planks of the floor.

My old bones, more likely, Melanie thought, though she was not yet old; not even by the saltier standards of the ocean-side towns strung like faded beads along the outermost strand of the Carolinas. But there was a certain wear to her, a fining down of the edges, and good wrinkles at the corners of her faded blue eyes. Not old, no, but sadly, no longer young, either.

Yet she looked comfortable in her skin. After much youthful turbulence, she found to her amazement that, while nothing had turned out as she'd hoped or expected, things had turned out fair enough in the end, and she with them.

Life was not perfect, but then, what life is? She bowed her head, her nostrils filling with the sweet childish scent of Merlyn's silk-fine hair, smiled and continued the murmured litany of the story.

'So on he went, deeper and deeper into the woods, until the wolf finally arrived at Grandmother's house . . .'

Her voice was husky, filled with the faintest remembrance of smoke.

Merlyn shivered in delicious anticipation (for children both love and fear the wolf), then squirmed in her mother's lap, twisting around to look up at Melanie's face. She made sure that Baby-Dolly, a white-capped, china-cheeked doll of uncertain age, was properly situated in the safety of her gangling, childish arms.

'That where Daddy is?' Merlyn asked, her voice a piping reed over the mutter of the fire. Outside, a dull wind began to stretch hollow fingers beneath the eaves, and Melanie imagined she perceived something beyond the wind – perhaps inside it. She paused, and in the silent interval heard rain, and the distant electric shout of a greater storm coming. She smiled at her own fancy and shook her head.

'Daddy'll be home soon, honey.'

Satisfied, Merlyn sank back down, clutching Baby-Dolly, and Melanie sighed as she absently rubbed the top of the little girl's head. She raised the storybook from which she was reading, though she didn't really need to. After a thousand repetitions, she had memorized the doings of the big bad wolf years ago.

'When he reached the door, the wolf looked around the forest to make sure he hadn't been seen. Then . . .'

Knock! knock!

The heavy, thudding sounds of knuckles slamming wood ripped apart the soft veil of the moment, and it was gone forever. Melanie turned towards the door, consternation on her features, her pale denim gaze suddenly sharp, worried.

The knock on the door in the night. She knew that sound from before.

Little Merlyn, still clutching Baby-Dolly, slid down from her mother's lap with childish eagerness and scrambled across the room to the big oak door as another fusillade of pounding shook the breathless silence. Merlyn flung the door open wide, then peered up at the giant man in the brown sheriff's uniform who loomed over her.

'Hello, darlin',' Lucas Buck boomed. 'Your mother here?'

Melanie Temple felt a spasm of absolute terror shriek up her spine.

Slowly, Merlyn turned, one of Baby-Dolly's little shoes scraping, unheeded and innocent, on the floor. 'Mama? Someone's at the door . . .'

Melanie half rose from the chair, the fingers of her right hand moving instinctively, protectively, to her neck. Her voice deepened, scratchy with fear. 'What do you want here?' she said.

But she knew . . .

'You know what I want,' Lucas shot back at her. 'We talked about it . . .'

He was a tall, lean man, his hair that indeterminate shade between chocolate and caramel, harsh lines stroked in his handsome face. There was cruelty to him; he carried himself with that raw certainty that frightens men and, sometimes, attracts women. The arrogance of control, of power nearly absolute; and the ability to conceal the inevitable corruption that such power always attends.

She raised her hands, palms out, in a warding gesture as she spun away from him, shaking her head. Her long hair flowed like melted gold in the firelight. 'Now I told you that you should stay away from me . . .'

10

But he moved on her quickly, as certain and contained as the storm rising beyond the door, coming for her. 'This isn't about you.' His eyes had gone dark and feral, and she could smell a sharp, acrid odour baking off him.

'Please . . . just stay away.' She hadn't meant to plead, had told herself she would never plead with Lucas Buck again. She'd believed that time long past, and now she cursed herself for a fool. He'd told her he would come. Hadn't he?

'It's about me.' And he was on her. 'It's about . . . *family*.'

As that once loved, now hated, and forever familiar embrace engulfed her, she hauled off and slapped him as hard as she could. The power of her blow stung her palm and tingled up her arm, and she might as well have slapped a boulder on the sea cliffs beyond the town.

By the open door, little Merlyn stood on the dark hem of the storm. Her eyes were wide as wounds. She shook with terror as her mother began to scream.

He had come with the beginning of the storm, and now he rode and broke her in the heart of it. And when he lifted himself up from her, the lightning burst around him like hand grenades, and the thunder punctuated his harsh breathing.

She stared up from her place of ruin on the floor,

her mind a blank and empty thing, one hand flung to the right, fingers curled, palm open and vulnerable. Her thighs ached from his frenzied, brutal assault.

'Why . . . ?' Such a stupid question, she thought. A weak question, and irrelevant to boot. Who cares why? Lucas Buck just is, and doesn't answer or explain. But a flicker of anger stirred. Later, she knew, it would be rage, but by then even the greater emotion would be futile. For now, she would settle for the anger, and demand her answers.

'Why?' she whispered again as he stood over her, smiling faintly, buckling his heavy leather gun belt around the rude ledges of his hips.

'Get up off the floor, Mellie,' he said. 'Ain't nothing more ridiculous-looking than a woman in your . . . position. Besides, that little girl of yours looks like she's about to have a fit.'

By the door, spatters of rain darkened a wide swath on the old wooden planks, and in that fan of shadow, Merlyn stood transfixed. Her eyes reflected the fire in chips of flickering red as she tried to cram her right fist wholly into her mouth. Baby-Dolly lay wet and dead-looking at her feet.

'Oh, my god, my baby . . .' Melanie gasped as she heaved herself up, absently straightening her dress and brushing a wild strand of hair from her face.

'Oh, Merlie, baby darling . . .'

She flung herself across the room and grabbed for the girl, the better to save her daughter or herself she couldn't tell. Merlie felt chilled, her skin pallid and damp with sweat. Like old meat.

She couldn't take her eyes from the spectre of Lucas Buck, who padded up behind and said, 'Little girl, don't you worry. Ain't nothing happened here to hurt you, nothing at all.'

That was when Merlyn Temple began to scream, and she never really stopped as long as she lived.

Chapter Two

TRINITY, SOUTH CAROLINA: 1972

Lucas Buck stood over the open grave, a sardonic smile vaguely twisting his otherwise respectful expression. Not ten feet away his father, Christopher Buck, preacher of the First Trinity Southern Baptist Church, raised his impressive, white-crowned profile and roared, *'Dust unto dust . . .'*

Yeah, yeah, Lucas thought. But I wonder if old Sydney figured he was going to eat dust as quick as he did?

Old Sydney, who was really nineteen-year-old Sydney Carpenter, fresh off a journey via body bag from a distant Asian place called Vietnam or, as it was pronounced within the environs of Trinity, 'Veet-nam', made no effort to reply. Which, Lucas told himself, was just as well; although the image of Sydney Carpenter suddenly sitting up in his coffin, turning eyes like dirty hard-boiled eggs on the gathered mourners and other hypocrites, and shouting, 'Hey, wait a minute! Changed my mind! Decided to dodge the draft after all! Shoulda been kissing boys instead of girls, back then!' was enough to make it hard to keep a properly straight face.

Well, he would anyway. Lucas Buck at that particular moment believed in no formal religion of any kind. Hard-shell Baptists, fish-sucking Catholics, Methodists, Jews, Muslims, none of them offered him any attraction. But he understood them, and understood that most varieties of religious folk would happily grind his bones into blasphemous red mush for even the sins he only contemplated, let alone the ones he'd already tried. Thus he wore whatever belief seemed appropriate and likely to avoid causing unnecessary animosity. Today, the Baptists got the garland.

He doubted Sydney gave much of a damn, either. Sydney, who'd started raising hell early when he'd had to whip a fair amount of fourth grade butt over the funny little cap his daddy wore on Saturdays, had been pretty quick to defend his old man, but pretty slow to pay much attention to Trinity's only synagogue.

Hence Preacher Buck doing the burying. Sydney's daddy had disowned him even before he'd joined the army, and hadn't changed his mind just because Sydney had come back in a military Hefty Bag. And Lucas knew the rumours about

Sydney joining up just ahead of a long vacation in the state penitentiary were more truth than falsehood. He should; he had helped to fix that small problem for good buddy Sydney.

Just then a thought flickered, like a shining fish breaking water, in the cool depths of Lucas's mind. His mental hands closed over it with lightning speed, and when he had it still, he looked within to see what he had caught.

Interesting. Out along the highway, just beyond the bridge, two indistinct figures. He could see the sign approaching: You Are Leaving Trinity, Population 9,657. Thanks For Visiting, Y'All Come Again.

He knew that spot of phoney southern hospitality well enough (it was also a notorious local speed trap) and had driven past it a thousand times in the six years since he'd been fourteen and started sneaking his first illegal joyrides.

The vision began to come a little clearer. He couldn't exactly explain, even to himself, just how he did this. Things came to him. It took him a long time to understand that this wasn't normal, that everybody else didn't have this disconcerting ability to *see* things.

A boy and a girl, a little younger than himself. He didn't know the boy. Long-haired kid. But the girl was Mellie Hankings, younger sister of Christine Hankings, who had married the newspaper owner Peter Emory back six, eight years ago.

Mellie Hankings was from the wrong side of the Chesapeake and Ohio railroad tracks, but she was a cute little thing and a local girl, and the thought of her heading out of town with some ugly hippy stranger didn't sit well with Lucas. Almost like a personal insult, as if she were sneaking out on him instead of the town.

He stuck his hands in his pockets and began to fidget. His father was still in full cry. Once Preacher Buck got to roaring and raring and shouting to Christ, he could go an easy couple of hours without ever drawing a full breath.

Have to do something about that, Lucas thought. Would be awful nice if one of those spring storms that come up out of nowhere decided to come up just about now . . .

He leaned back slightly and began to scan the empty blue horizon expectantly.

Sure enough, within a couple of minutes he saw the first ragged grey wisps poke up in the hazy distance. Must have been a good wind behind them, because they darkened swiftly, swelling into huge hammer heads of lightning-frazzled cumulus.

Others began to glance around nervously, as the sound of muted thunder grew closer. A brisk breeze sprang up, scattering the remnants of last autumn's leaves. A few dusted across Sydney's coffin, looking sad and out of place.

The first heavy spatters thumped onto the

rounded copper top of the coffin, sounding like fingers on spectral bongo drums. Now the breeze turned gusty, ripping at the red-and-white striped awning that protected the grave and the portable podium where Preacher Buck paused, looked up, took a breath, then shook his head.

He leaned over the podium and gathered the small crowd into his gaze. 'I know you good folks want to do a proper job of paying your last respects to this poor boy, but I'm sure he'd understand.'

The preacher tilted his head in the direction of the two grave diggers who leaned against a small backhoe parked behind the makeshift pavilion. 'May the dear departed rest in eternal peace, fast in the bosom of the Lord.' He nodded again.

'Boys, it's done. Take her on down.'

The bottoms of the clouds opened as the mourners scrambled for their cars. Preacher Buck ran awkwardly, holding his Bible over his head, the tail of his light blue Sears and Roebuck no-iron-needed sport coat flapping behind him as he headed for a firehouse-red Pontiac GTO convertible with a white top. He piled in next to his son.

'We did Sydney up right, don't you think, Lucas?' He grinned widely. 'Not that he gave that much of a damn, I bet you. Boy raised more hell than even you ever dreamed of. Still, I'd sorta like to see the town put up some kind of memorial for our boys. He's the third already.' He nodded, musing, perhaps imagining the dedication speech he could make.

'Something nice, in the middle of the town square, over by the War Memorial. Got those pretty moss oak trees, y'know? Make a nice shady spot.'

In Trinity, world wars, Germans, Japs, and Commies might come and go, but there was still only one conflict called the War, and though it had ended in 1865, there were people around more than willing to take another crack at it.

Lucas cranked the big engine, jerked the Hurst shifter forward into first, and left chunks of cemetery sod spinning in his wake. Preacher Buck bounced off the back of his leather seat, both his hands going forward for leverage against the dashboard.

'You in some kind of a hurry, boy, or is it you just don't like funerals?'

Lucas turned his head slightly, his expression even more sardonic. "'Bout as much as you do, Daddy. Can I drop you at the parsonage?'

'Why, that would be nice, son. This rain. You know my petunias are like to all be washed away. Funny rain, come up so quick like that. You'd almost think God didn't want us to get Sydney buried proper.'

'You might,' Lucas agreed. 'If you believed in God.'

He glanced over at his father, who now folded

his big hands piously over his considerable paunch. 'Good thing,' Lucas went on, 'that neither one of us has that little problem.'

Preacher Buck cleared his throat. 'My petunias, Lucas. Now don't forget my poor petunias.'

By the time Lucas pulled up at the whitewashed curb in front of the Baptist parsonage's neatly hedged front lawn, the spring squall had faded as if it had never been. A gentle breeze rustled the tender green leaves of two ancient oaks that guarded the front porch of the trim little shingled house. But overhead the sky had begun to shade into that blank glaring white colour that meant the rest of the day would turn as hot as a fourth of July firecracker.

'Here you go, Daddy. I think your petunias lucked out after all.'

Preacher Buck swiped a bright blue bandana across his sweating forehead. He felt hot, sticky, and vaguely irritated with his son and this damned big car he drove. Buffeted and uncomfortable, and he couldn't get it out of his craw that Lucas was somehow mocking him. Preacher Buck regarded himself as a reasonable, even a kindly man, but he couldn't bear to be mocked, not even by his own blood.

Especially by his own blood.

But none of this showed on his florid features as

he slid his ample rear towards his door, pushed it open, and clambered out onto the blacktop. He paused, wheezing, and swabbed his forehead again as he bent over to peer back into the interior.

'I suppose you're taking off somewhere?'

Lucas regarded him blankly. 'Sure am, Daddy.'

Preacher Buck waited one long beat to see if further information might be forthcoming, but when all Lucas did was push the button that started the convertible top motor to whining, he shook his head and stood back.

'Kids used to have more respect for their elders,' he muttered as he turned away.

Lucas chuckled sharply.

Preacher Buck whirled, astonishingly agile for a man pushing hard on fifty and trying to pretend that his trousers fastened around his belly just as easy as they had ten years ago. 'Something I said, boy? You want to share the joke with your old daddy?'

Lucas speared him with a glance. 'Maybe some still do, you know? But I kinda doubt the Buck men have ever had that luxury. Of respecting our daddies, know what I mean?'

Preacher Buck did, exactly and precisely, so he broke off the charade as gracefully as he could.

'You coming for dinner next Thursday like usual? I got some of the winter lamb old Deacon Brooks killed off last week. Marie found some fresh mint, she's all hot to roast up a leg or two.'

Lucas nodded. Marie Fairthingale was his father's maid, a formidable old biddy despite the delicate French overtones of her name, though she cooked like all the angels in heaven. 'Sounds good, Daddy. You can count on me.'

The canvas top finished its faintly menacing crablike contraction into the well behind the rear seat. When Lucas was sure it was firmly settled he whipped the big chrome shifter ball forward, floored the gas pedal, and popped the clutch.

The result was twenty feet of smoking rubber stripes on the Preacher's pristine blacktop that got the Preacher to shaking his head and wondering what the world was coming to.

Coming to hell in a handbasket, most likely. In Preacher Buck's experience, that was usually the case. At least as long as he could remember.

He exhaled heavily and trudged across the sidewalk towards the freshly painted gate in his low picket fence. Best to check on those petunias anyway. You never could tell . . .

Damn that boy.

If it was not the stupidest thing she'd ever done in her life, Melanie Hankings told herself, it had to be right up there. But stupid or not, it looked pretty certain she was going to end up stuck with it anyway. Stuck with Larry Something-or-other, that is. Here she was, leaving the town she'd been born in and grown up in, heading north with some guy and she didn't even know his last name.

Stupid, stupid, stupid.

'What'd you say?' Larry asked.

She moved her shoulders. 'Didn't say nothing,' she told him.

They'd run back and tossed their duffel bags under the rusty old girders that held up the north end of the bridge, where everything smelled of dank water and dead fish, to wait out the storm. As they crossed back over the Trinity city line, Mellie felt a twinge, as if somebody had stroked fingertips across the base of her spine very lightly and very quickly. Goose on my grave, she thought, and shivered. Then the rain really started to come down, and she forgot about it.

Now, as they climbed slowly back to the road, the puddles of rainwater were already beginning to steam, sunlight blistering off them so bright it made you want to squint. Heat mirages danced above the pavement out ahead, far as the eye could see, till they vanished in the thick green oaks that lined the road. Overhead, the sky was turning that vague pale colour, like a door slowly opening on a vast, idiot furnace.

That kind of sky always made her feel like a helpless bug squirming on a griddle, waiting for God's heel to come down and squash her into mush.

My, what a fine self-image you've got for

yourself, girl, she thought. You keep on reading those psychology books, no telling what you'll dream up next . . . bug on a griddle, no shit.

'I thought I heard something,' Larry insisted. 'You call me stupid?'

'No, I didn't call you stupid.' *Called myself stupid, though, but it's not the same thing. Is it?*

He looked at her out of the corners of his eyes. It was an expression that she was already getting a little tired of. He would be looking at her straight on, but then he would slowly turn to the side, stick his nose up just a hitch, and roll his eyeballs as if he'd stepped in something that smelled funny. It had been cute at first, but was growing less endearing by the second.

'Larry, don't look at me that way. I ain't something on the bottom of your shoe, you dig?'

'I'm not looking at you some way. What are you talking about, babe? I think this southern sun has fried your brains a little. Unless it's all this good Dixie dope. You wanna smoke a joint, Mellie?'

He reached into the chest pocket of his jeans jacket and half-fumbled out his stash before she managed to blurt, 'Have you lost your entire mind, boy?'

'Huh?'

'This isn't your New York City, Larry, or any of them other Yankee places where they cut you a little slack. You get caught with that shit down here, you'll be doing time on some chain gang chopping weeds and dodging water moccasins for the next twenty years. The pigs down here, they don't fool around, you hear me?'

He paused, a petulant expression on his thin, too-wide lips (teeth kinda mossy, too, she noted), then pushed the little leather bag back into his pocket. 'Huh. I keep forgetting I'm not in civilization anymore.'

She looked away from him, hoping he hadn't seen the expression she'd felt flicker on her own features. She had every reason – far more reason than some tourist Yankee hippy – to hate the South, and Trinity in particular. Still, his sneering attitude got right under her skin and made her think that maybe there was such a thing, in this new Age of Aquarius, as *too much* peace and love. Maybe old Larry just needed a swat in the patootie. Common him down a bit. Southern boys might be horny pigs, but in general their manners were a good sight better than the average Yankee.

Evidently what she'd said had miffed him a little, because he walked right on ahead five or six good paces before he slowed, but he maintained the distance between them.

Put me in my place, she thought. There was a movement gaining steam up north, some woman named Betty Friedan, a lot of talk about women's rights, and that was one of the reasons she intended to shake Trinity's dust from her heels and do something right for the first time in her whole life. She read a lot, for a girl from the other side of the C&O tracks, and she knew about things.

She knew, for instance, that good old Larry, walking ahead of her and probably well aware that his butt looked OK in those greasy tight bell-bottom jeans, was at best a temporary condition. She thought of him as a ticket – she'd never done any real hitching on her own, and figured it would be better to learn how those particular ropes got untangled with a partner, rather than all by her lonesome.

With only one exception, the history of the Hankings family was an unrelieved string of fail-ures brought on by booze and violence and ignorance and plain, simple despair. The excep-tion was her older sister, Christine, who had not been able to escape Trinity, but had been able to unshackle herself from the dreary inevitability of waitressing and getting knocked up and marrying some Timmy or Joey or even Sydney, then calving every year like clockwork while Timmy or Joey whacked her around whenever she didn't deliver the cans of Pearl beer cold enough or quick enough.

Chrissy had graduated from Trinity High – an accomplishment for any Hankings, male or female, in its own right – then married Peter Emory, whose daddy left him both money and git-up-and-go, and now Peter Emory owned the town newspaper, the *Trinity Guardian*.

There were no kids yet, not even after five years of trying, and Mellie knew that was a secret sorrow to Chrissy. But even so, Chrissy had broken the dismal string, and Mellie intended to make it two in a row for the Hankings girls. And maybe if she could pull off that unvarnished miracle, it would help a little to make up for Stephen Hankings, but that was another story entirely, and she didn't want to think about it anymore. Stephen Hankings was yet another reason for her to hate Trinity. Or God, or fate, one of the three.

Besides, for the last couple of years or so, she'd been having bad dreams, shapeless fiery things she couldn't remember when she'd jerk up suddenly awake all sweaty and bulgy-eyed, breathing like a good quarter horse after a couple of laps around the fairgrounds track. The dreams had something to do with the town – the town, and somebody in it, though for the life of her she couldn't figure out who.

Not that it mattered, she thought as she watched Larry Whatsisname walk his macho little strut up ahead, showing off for his chick. What was he, about seventeen? And thinks he's walking the walk. Hell, more like talking the walk. Larry was real good at talking, a regular silver-tongued devil.

She snorted softly. Men.

Odd thing, though. Not a single car had come by since the storm. And though she'd expected to feel a lot better the farther she got from the city limits, in fact, she was growing uneasier with each step she took. And the duffel bag balanced across her shoulders was starting to feel like she'd packed it with a couple of anvils.

She paused, turned, and looked back down the road. She'd been a good bible-reading Baptist when she was younger, and for a moment the tale of Lot's wife ghosted through her thoughts. Huh, pretty funny, pillar of salt at the edge of State Highway 129. Nothing back there anyway to look back at, no Sodom nor Gomorrah, either.

So what, all of a sudden, was she so scared of? It wasn't her time of the month, so she couldn't blame it on that, even if waving the red flag made her flighty, which it didn't. And the bridge had almost vanished in the distance.

She turned back around and saw that Larry had stopped.

'What's up, babe? You homesick already?'

She shrugged. 'Not hardly,' she told him.

In the muffled, muggy distance, a big engine, whining on the redline. Coming fast.

'You know, I betcha that's our ride,' Larry said.

Lucas Buck loved that big red convertible. Just like Mellie Hankings, he read books too, and he knew all about those weird theories concerning men and their cars and their dicks. Well, hell, give him a pud that ran 420 horsepower, he'd take that baby any day of the week and twice on Sundays. Fool psychologists generally had their heads up their collective psyches, anyway.

He downshifted from second to first, unleashing a sudden *rappopparrapp* of hot exhaust – a sound so characteristic of the monster engine of the GTO that he privately thought of it as goat farts. He came to an idling halt at the corner of Oleander and South College and tapped the accelerator as he waited for the light to turn, getting off on the powerful throb of the engine and half chuckling as he thought what those shrinks would say about that.

'Yo, Lucas!'

'That you, Ben?'

Ben Healy waved from where he sat cross-legged on top of the crumbling stone retainer wall that kept most of Hogtown Hill from falling into Oleander Drive. He had a brown paper bag in his lap, twisted at the top, just about the right size for a cold quart of Pearl. Ben Healy was four years younger than Lucas, proud as hell of the brand new learner's permit in his battered wallet, deeply in lust with Lucas's GTO, and willing to follow Lucas to hell and back if it might someday put him behind the wheel, even for a moment, of that awesome vehicle.

'Where you headed? Can I come along?' Without waiting for an answer he slid off the wall

29

and landed on his Keds, being careful to keep a tight grip on his paper bag.

'That wouldn't be some illegal beer, would it?' Lucas asked mildly.

'Sure is. Want some?' Ben passed the bag across the empty shotgun seat. 'Where we going?' he asked.

'I haven't said I'm taking you anywhere. You're just a kid, Ben.' He swallowed and wiped his lips on the back of his hand. 'Got good beer, though, even if you are a minor. Come on, get your raggedy butt in here.'

'All right!' Grinning, Ben didn't bother with opening the door, just put his palm on the window-sill and cleared it with one good jump.

'Boy, you mess up my leather upholstery and I'll patch it with your hide,' Lucas said.

Ben looked down. 'Looks OK to me. Got clean jeans on, anyway. So where we going?'

The light changed. Lucas dropped the shifter and popped the clutch. The usual screech, smoke, and sharp stink of fried rubber followed, accompanied by a rebel yell from Ben.

'Yeaagghhh!'

'Ride'm cowboy,' Lucas said. 'Hey, Ben, you got any more of that beer stashed somewhere? Say you do, we'll stop for that, and then I think we'll take us a ride out of town a ways.'

* * *

'What did you think you were going to do with six quarts of Pearl, Ben? Drink 'em all? You'd be walking on your ass and elbows for a month.'

Ben shrugged. The wind riffled his thin blond hair, so fine you could see the pink scalp underneath. Lucas never said so, but he thought Ben would most likely go pretty near to bald by thirty. The way his hairline already arched up high in front just sort of hinted at more drastic changes to come.

'Beer's beer. Somebody's always willing to help you drink it.'

'How'd you pay for it?'

'Mowed a bunch of lawns this weekend. Made about twenty bucks all told.'

Lucas shook his head appreciatively. 'Man, that's a lot of grass. Even for a good cause like beer.'

'I'm saving to get me a car.' Ben turned shyly away. 'Want me a goat, just like yours.'

'Well, hey, Ben . . .' Lucas didn't quite know what to say. He didn't have the heart to tell the kid he could buy a brand new Caddy for what Lucas had put into this version of the Buckmobile. And he doubted Ben would ever develop anything like his own talent for making money out of the oddest deals. Like Sydney Carpenter, for instance, whose father owned the big GM dealership out south of town and who, for some reason, thought

Lucas deserving of some pretty amazing credit and down payment terms. Old man might have disowned his son, but underneath he didn't really want to see the boy in the state pen.

In the distance, sunlight glinted viciously off the top girders of the River Bridge. Lucas raised his foot off the accelerator pedal a bit. 'Say, Ben, you know the Hankings family at all?'

Ben had one fist buried deep in a bag of Red Man Potato Chips. There was a trail of orange-red crumbs running down the front of his Trinity Gophers T-shirt when he looked up.

'Huh? Sure. Well, I know Melanie. Just to say hi to, you know. She's my age, but she keeps to herself. Kinda strange for Hankings girls, you know what I mean?'

'No, Ben. What do you mean?'

Ben shrugged, a little embarrassed. 'Well, that family. I mean, you knew the older girl, that Christine that married the owner of the paper? She woulda been about your age, right?'

'Uh huh. Nice girl, seemed like. A little snooty, maybe, for somebody from that side of the tracks.'

'Yeah, just what I mean,' Ben said eagerly. 'Mellie, she's like that, too. Like she's better than most folks? But hell, that whole family, daddy, momma, aunts, uncles and cousins – all I can say is, if Mellie Hankings is snooty, it's something she does on her own. Family's nothing but plain old swamp-jumping, hardscrabble white trash,

32

back about fifty generations, I guess.'

Lucas leaned back against the soft red leather and squinted at the tanglework of iron beams coming up fast in front of him. He slowed her down almost to a crawl as he crossed the bridge. Ben peered over the side at a big wooden raft anchored out in the river. He waved his quart of Pearl at several kids of various ages lounging, diving, swimming, and generally raising summer hell around the raft. It was early in the season, and most of the tans were the kind where arms and knees were dark, but the shirt lines hadn't quite blended in yet.

'Yaooo!'

'Hold your water, Ben. You going to act like a kid, I'm going to pitch you over the side with the rest of them.' Lucas came to a halt right at the city line. 'No deputy dawgs hiding out here today,' he noted. 'Musta already got their quota for the week.'

'Why you want to know about the Hankings? Didn't you used to know Steve, before, uh, you know?'

Lucas nodded. 'Yeah, I knew Steve. Damn shame about that, too. Anyway, can you figure out why Mellie Hankings, sixteen same as you, would be leaving town with some straggly-ass long haired Yankee hippy?'

'What?'

'That's what I'm telling you, Ben, and in just

a couple of minutes, I'm going to show you.'

And with that, Lucas slapped the pedal to the metal and the big GTO blasted out away from the bridge like an old yellow dog with a cherry bomb up its tail.

Chapter Three

Lawrence Arthur Rosenweig. That was his name. He would have died rather than admit to the Arthur part of it, because the path from Arthur to Artie was short but hideous, and the possibility of being *Artie* Rosenweig was well and truly beyond even thinking about. On the other hand, Larry had a nice goyish sound to it, and he was pretty sure that when he was introduced as just plain old Larry, people treated him somehow differently than if he was revealed as Larry Rosenweig. Not as bad as Artie Rosenweig, maybe, and it wasn't anything he could put his finger on, but he knew it was there. His mother would have said it was his instincts talking, with an arch lift to her perfectly shaped and plucked eyebrows, hinting at decades of persecution, personally suffered.

Larry knew the worst thing that had ever happened to his mother was being forced to move from New York City, which contained Saks Fifth Avenue, B. Altman, Lord and Taylor, and Cartier, and settle in Middletown, Indiana, where the biggest store was called the Globe Department Store, after the Globe fruit jar family who more or less owned Middletown.

Martha Rosenweig had not exactly lived a life of deprivation, although she would probably have viewed it differently. Larry was the youngest of three – he had two older sisters – and when he was born his mother, as if she had completed her side of some unspoken bargain with Larry's father, Milton, by supplying him with a boy child, took to her bed. She would not rise from it till Larry's bar mitzvah, shortly after he turned thirteen. To this day he somehow still got her all mixed up with the story about Lazarus, even though the genders were wrong.

The oddest thing was that his father, Milton, had not seemed to mind. Larry had no idea what went on at night in that perpetually dim and shadowy conjugal bedroom his mother never left, but Milton seemed happy enough with it. He had his own life anyway, an odd amalgam of the mind and the corporate world, wherein he used the fruits of his Ph.D. in philosophy to study the teachings of the ancients by night, snug in his well-appointed den with the big stereo system playing Mozart. During the day he waged war from his office at the Arca paper mill he'd inherited from *his* father, a jumble of sheds, warehouses, and incomprehensible machinery down by the DuBlanc River, two miles away.

As far as Larry could tell, Milton was satisfied with life in general and Middletown in particular. Even though his house, one of the largest in town, was situated across Creekside Drive from Brentwood Estates. When he had set out to build his place, he had been unable to find a lot for sale over there in the Estates. Not that there *weren't* any lots, just that the ones that did exist – at least five – weren't for sale. Not to Milton Rosenweig, at any rate. His money was just – heh, heh – no good.

So Milton had brought in a big-time architect from New York and put up one of those houses made out of redwood from California and smoky sheet glass custom poured in Pittsburgh, and limestone – his only concession to regional industry – from Indiana, from the quarries south of Indianapolis.

Everybody said they admired the place, although Larry noticed that none of his friends lived in anything like it, nor did they give any hint of ever intending to do so.

Martha rose from her bed just in time to see her eldest daughter married off to a nice young man she had met at Columbia University. It is debatable whether it was the union itself – or the chance for Martha to take off for six months to New York to help the newlyweds get settled in – that brought her unexpected resurrection. Larry remembered wondering if this was just some new, long-distance version of maternal purdah, and was surprised to find he didn't much care. By then, he was beginning to have his own problems. Most of them, it seemed to him, revolved around his last name.

Anti-semitism, in the middle Sixties in Indiana, was not the naked and brutal affair it had been a generation before, when the Kluckers openly ruled the state government, and hated niggers, kikes, and papists with equal vigour. But as Larry slowly grew to a more encompassing level of social awareness, he realized that while he could sit in any restaurant he pleased, and ride any public conveyance, even take a whiz in any restroom that wasn't locked, he could not go swimming, other than as a guest, at the Lincoln County Country Club.

Oh, his father could easily afford the fees, but, as the jolly saying went, his money wasn't – heh, heh – any good there. It was fine at the Rolling Hills Golf Club – though oddly enough most of his non-Jewish friends never seemed to be able to go swimming with him there, either. For a while he thought wildly that it was something in the water of the Rolling Hills pool; then he realized it was something in the air, more specifically in an understanding of the way the world really was, as viewed by the parents and grandparents of the children he knew.

Rosenweig. His father was proud of the name. Larry hated it, and for five years after he turned thirteen, he promised himself he would do something about that. He turned thirteen in 1967, when the world was convulsing so strongly the waves were felt even in Middletown.

By the time the waves had receded somewhat, in 1972, Larry had hair down to his shoulders, a hole in his right ear he'd punched with a carpet needle one night while he was drunk on half a case of Pabst Blue Ribbon beer and high on six hits of white cross speed (in which he wore a round gold hoop earring that drove Milton purely crazy), and an abiding interest in going any place he could find where he could be just plain old Larry. Preferably a place where, if he ever did come by any money, it would always be – heh, heh – good as goddamned gold.

Which had brought him to this oak-shaded state highway a couple of miles north of Trinity, South Carolina, where he was contemplating the idea that he might have fucked up all over again.

It was the big red GTO, vanishing into the heat mirages further on towards what his creased Shell Oil road map said was a shit-kicker burg called Ascension, that brought him to this consideration.

'Sonofabitch,' he said very calmly, because the shock hadn't really set into his brain yet – though from the cottage-cheese colour his face had blanched to, his body had a pretty fair idea of what was going on. Nevertheless, there was the sound of genuinely innocent surprise in his voice – and a little shakiness, too – as he whooshed out a breath and then said, 'Mellie, am I wrong, or did that sucker just try to kill me?'

Her gaze was distant, somewhere off down the road. 'That was Lucas Buck's car. You better get yourself ready, I guess.'

'Why's that?'

'Cause he'll be back.'

'Now what in the hell did you think you were *doin'* back there, Ben?' Lucas said.

Ben heard that familiar tone in Lucas's voice, and gave himself over to a bit of prudent thought before he replied. Finally, slowly, he said, 'I dunno, Lucas. Just seemed like the thing to do. At the time, I mean. I sorta thought you would be OK with it.'

'With what, Ben? With throwin' a half full bottle of Pearl at some hitchhiker's skull? You could of killed that boy, and then what? Think anybody wouldn't have noticed this car? That *was* Melanie Hankings back there with him, wasn't it? Or were you planning to bash in *her* skull, too?'

Ben shook his head. He lived a life oddly torn, for a respectable white southern boy. His father was the Deputy Fire Chief of the Trinity Fire Department, had been as long as anybody could remember. And everybody who knew anything about it knew that Carlton Healy had gone as far as he could.

Fire Chief was an elective position, and though folks thought Carlton was the best of good old boys, he had a skunk's chance in a perfume factory of being elected dog catcher, let alone Fire Chief. Carlton, it was said, was born to be a follower, and general sentiment had it his son was most likely going to tread in those very same footsteps.

Ben Healy knew all this as well as he knew how many toes he had on both feet, and he also knew that somehow he was going to make all the gossiping old biddies wrong. Only problem was, at sixteen, he hadn't quite figured out how he was going to do it. But the extremely complex set of feelings that came over him every time he was around Lucas Buck had just about convinced him that his star, whatever it was going to be, was tied to the dark, saturnine boy in the driver's seat next to him.

This secret knowledge was both a comfort – usually – and a worry – occasionally. Oh, not that he had any doubt Lucas would be a big success in Trinity (strangely, the idea that Lucas might *leave* Trinity to find his future had never so much as crossed Ben's mind), but he still couldn't quite figure out how all this was going to come about.

He possessed that kind of fatalistic wariness natural in a boy who, three years before, had been surprised beneath his blankets by his mother, while occupied with a flashlight and a bootleg copy of *Playboy* he'd hawked from the rack in the rear of Grisham's Drug Store that morning. His mother had ripped off the blanket, averted her eyes from the rest of it as she snatched away the *Playboy*, and dragged him down to Preacher Buck the next day. After first scrubbing, then *boiling*, his sheets and jockey shorts.

She obviously didn't think her easygoing husband would be vigorous enough at thwarting this advance of the devil upon the body of her only son. After that experience, Ben assumed the worst would generally happen, but he worried about it anyway, kind of damned if he did, and damned any other way, too.

'I'm sorry, Lucas,' he said. 'Didn't mean nothing. Wasn't aiming to hit him anyway.' He glanced over. 'So what are we gonna do?'

'About what, Ben? You want to go back there and apologize?'

'Well, of course not,' Ben replied. 'No harm done, and besides, he's just some hippy root-sucker. What's he doing with Mellie, though, I wonder?'

Lucas sighed, downshifted quickly, yanked the steering wheel all the way to the right, and threw the big convertible into a full sliding three sixty. It was an impressive bit of driving, but, unexpected as it was, Ben felt a nasty bubble of half-digested Pearl beer burping up into his throat.

Without looking at him, Lucas said, 'You puke in my car, I'll tear your head off and use your hair for a mop.'

Ben splayed the fingers of his right hand delicately over his lips. His eyes were round as warning signals at a C&O crossing. He nodded once, carefully. And kept the beer down.

Lucas put half of his mind on the hot, sweaty delight of the big car winding up beneath him, but the other half began to fizz with the kind of expectancy he hadn't felt since, four years before, he met the twenty-five-year-old widow librarian, Angela Harsfeldt, and she began to show him some things that, as she put it, weren't written in the books. At least, not the books you could put your hands on in the Trinity Public Library.

Back then, though he was no virgin even in those days, whenever he'd even think about Angela, a bubbly kind of heat would start in the V of his groin and work its way into a full-blown furnace behind his navel. The real Angela, in the almost too pliant flesh, was one amazing surprise after another. Comparing her to local girls like Selena Coombs – though Selena made up in vigour and willingness and sheer sensual *heat* for what she lacked in experience – was in the order of choosing between, he imagined, caviar and chicken fried steak.

(Although he loved chicken fried steak, and had never tasted caviar in his whole life, Lucas assumed that the caviar would have to taste better, on reputation alone if for no other reason. When, later in life, he discovered this was not the case, it would become one of the foundations of his awesome cynicism.) But it wasn't so much the act of sex with Angela as the anticipation of it that really turned his crank, and got that big deep engine inside him grumbling and growling.

And that big hairy crank was turning and burning right now, as he aimed the GTO like a fire truck missile back down the road towards Trinity.

Ben fished a rusty church key out of his jeans pocket and popped another bottle of Pearl. The stuff was nearly lukewarm by now, but any southern boy who couldn't drink warm beer most likely didn't get drunk at all. He looked a lot less green around the gills, though his high forehead already showed sunburn the colour of half-ripe cherries. Lucas knew it would start to peel soon, and Ben, as usual, would walk around all summer with his face coming loose in big white patches that made a soft, whispery-sticky sound when he peeled them away.

'Ben?'

'Huh? What, Lucas?'

'You let me handle this, OK?'

'Sure, Lucas. We gonna whip that Yankee boy's ass?'

Lucas shrugged. 'Don't know yet, Ben. Depends.'

'Depends on what?'

Lucas slid his hazel eyes in Ben's direction and winked slowly. 'Oh, you know,' he said. 'Whatever's going.'

Ben nodded. He didn't know, but he'd seen this kind of thing before. A little shivery thrill twitched at his shoulder blades, even with the afternoon sun burning down on the back of his neck. Whenever Lucas got into one of these moods, somebody, in some way, usually ended up in a world of hurt.

It scared him and elated him at the same time, and he didn't know how he felt about that. He wondered who was in for trouble. The hippy boy? Or Melanie?

The answer seemed obvious enough, but with Lucas you could never tell – and maybe that was half the fun. Then, in the distance, on the left-hand side of the road, barely visible in the shimmering mirage of heat, two figures.

Growing closer.

Ben held on tight as Lucas blasted past the pair once again, then pulled another of those incredible U-turns, smoking like a dervish on the soft blacktop. He brought the car to a shuddering, thrumming halt on the pavement, right next to the hippy and Melanie Hankings.

'Afternoon,' Lucas said. 'You folks need a ride?'

The boy shaded his eyes with one hand and glared at him. 'That you, throwing beer bottles at me?'

Lucas grinned faintly. Something indefinable in his eyes changed just then, and Ben thought, *uh-oh* . . .

'What makes you think it was me, hippy boy? Might have been old Melanie here. That you, Melanie Hankings? You look a little like your older sister.'

She nodded. 'Hello, Lucas. We've met before, I think.'

'Huh? I thought I always remember a pretty girl, but I don't remember talking to you, darlin'.'

She smiled, and her whole face transformed from something prematurely tired and almost plain into what Lucas thought of as *a radiant lamp*, or some such biblical sounding thing. Just then the wind lifted her hair and it blazed out like a crown of burnished copper-gold. He felt the beat in the soft part of his throat begin to hammer gently.

'It was at the Methodist ice cream social last year, Lucas,' she said. 'You brought me a chunk of watermelon, and we sat and talked for a minute.'

A powerful surge of lust twisted his testicles as he stared at her, like nothing he'd ever experienced before, even with Angela Harsfeldt. Something there, deep inside her, calling to him. But careful,

46

because there was something else there, too, inextricably entwined with the part he lusted for.

It made him think of angels, and he didn't like that. But what the hell, in for a nickel, in for the whole load. It made it better, anyway. The spice of danger. Otherwise, it was just shooting little sixteen-year-old fish in a barrel, and although Lucas would take whatever came his way – gift horses never had to worry about him checking their teeth – this little Mellie Hankings was different. Something about her, a goodness, almost like a saint . . . The whole package was just incredibly attractive.

He let his grin widen. 'Sure I do, now that you mention it, Mellie. Hot July day, almost like this, and you were wearing cut-off jeans and a pretty blue blouse with the tails tied together so that your belly button showed. Sure I remember.'

She smiled, acknowledging that he had the details correct.

'Hey, that's sweet,' the hippy boy broke in. 'Old friends and all, cool. But we're headed north, friend. If you're going that way, we'd be happy for a ride.'

Ben winced. Slowly, Lucas turned his head. An uncertain expression wavered across Melanie's face, but Larry didn't see it.

'What's your name, boy?' Lucas said mildly.

When Larry had turned thirteen, not long after his bar mitzvah and his mother's abrupt departure for New York, a movie had come to Middletown that had made one hell of an impact, particularly amongst that group of professors and students on the campus of the Globe State Teachers College who were generally considered to be Commie pinko fags by the non-educational population of Middletown.

Called *In the Heat of the Night*, it starred Sydney Poitier as a black Philadelphia cop facing down a redneck southern sheriff played by one of those guys Larry knew was a very good actor, but whose name he could never remember. Rod something-or-other?

One of the big moments in the film was when the sheriff asked Sydney Poitier what they called him back in Philly, *boy*, and Poitier, the whites of his eyes seeming to spurt hellfire out of his black face, had replied, 'They call me *Mister* Tibbs.'

The line had always been good for cheers, whistles, and applause, and Larry wanted more than anything to put this southern cracker with the demonic grin in his place in similar fashion. Unfortunately, 'They call me *Mister* Rosenweig,' somehow didn't seem to offer the same impact.

He looked down at his scuffed boot toes for a second, then looked up, flipped his brown hair out of his face, and said, 'Larry. Why? You need me to fill out some kind of application to give me a ride?'

'No, no,' Lucas said. 'Larry. Just so I don't have to call you "hey, you". Tell you what, though,

Larry. There is something I do need from you, if you want me to give you a ride.'

Larry did that strange head-twisting, eye-rolling half sneer that Mellie really didn't like at all. 'Yeah? What's that?'

Lucas drummed his fingers on the top of the steering wheel for a moment, then shrugged. 'I need you to tell me something. Just what are you gonna give me, Larry, if I give you a ride?'

Larry stared at him. 'What the hell you talking about, man? What I give you?' He reached towards his right hip pocket. 'I got a little bread, you know. For gas money. That what you want?'

But Lucas, still shaking his head, his grin now even wider, but somehow flat and menacing, said, 'No, Larry. I got money and I buy my own gas. I mean, what can you give me? Looks to me like getting out of this part of the country might be real important to you, being a hippy boy from Yankee country. And with that funny name of yours and all.'

And with that, magically, a switchblade flicked open in Lucas's right hand. The chrome steel blade caught the sunlight and blinked ferociously. Ben sucked in a breath, closed his eyes, and slumped lower in his seat.

Dreamily, Lucas stared at the way the light rippled up and down the blade as he turned it back and forth at eye level. Glints of reflected light exploded off the dark planes of his cheekbones.

'Boys like you, they get cut anyway, right around thirteen or so? Huh, just about the time you can get it up, they go and cut some of it off. Ain't that the truth, Larry? But I don't want your money. Truth be told, Larry, your money just isn't – heh, heh – any good around here.'

'What do you want from me, *peckerwood*!'

Ben peered over the edge of the car window-sill. The hippy boy's face had gone red as a beet. Melanie was staring at him with mingled pity and confusion, but Lucas seemed completely unmoved by the effect he'd created. He kept on staring at his knife.

'Come on, Larry. Like the Beatles said, money can't buy you love. So what you got to offer for a ride back up north, where they like your kind of people, know how to treat them? Come on now, think quick!'

And with that, Lucas was out of the car and somehow standing right next to Larry Rosenweig, his right hand dangling down, loosely grasping the switchblade. Lucas made a slight movement and tapped the rounded bulge at the fork of Larry's jeans with the finely stropped edge of the blade. Larry flinched involuntarily.

'That bring back any memories, boy?' Lucas whispered. 'You thinking now?'

'Lucas!'

He turned slightly. 'Now, Melanie, if you don't want things to get entirely out of hand here, you might want to think about keeping quiet for a bit. Let me and Larry here get this thing figured out.'

Larry's face was bleached out pale as a bowl of whipping cream. Two dull red spots burned on his cheeks. He looked terrified enough to pass out, and mad enough to commit murder, all in the same expression. Ben thought it was a hell of a sight to see.

'What do you want from me?' Larry said.

'Why, whatever you got to give, son. Whatever's right. How about you telling me?'

With that, Lucas's gaze slid from Larry's frozen features until it rested on Melanie, her expression a mask of disgust as she stood poised to fight or run a few feet away.

Lucas smiled. 'You willing to trade . . . *her*, for instance?'

'Hey, man, you out of your fucking mind? I can't trade her for nothing, man. I don't own her. Hardly know her, as a matter of fact.'

Now Lucas put his face right next to Larry's. His lips had drawn back from his teeth, exposing canines that looked almost wolf-like, white as bleached bone. 'Oh, I think you do, Larry. I think what you can do is just give her to me, you know? Sort of . . . forfeit your rights. See, down here, Larry, you're just another ugly hippy boy, and a Yankee to boot. You don't belong, you know what I mean?'

Lucas, still grinning that devil's-head grin,

stepped back a pace. The blade of his knife flashed once in the sun as Larry jerked back out of the way. Not quickly enough, though; a small brown pouch fell to the road from the bottom of the pocket Lucas had halfway cut off Larry's jean jacket. And a sharp, acrid smell rose from the dark spot now spreading in Larry's crotch.

Larry bent down to grab for the stash, and narrowly missed getting his fingers crushed by Lucas's boot heel coming down.

'Now, now,' Lucas said. 'Let's not be hasty. And what have we got here?' He speared the bag with the point of his knife and flipped it into the air, catching it neatly with his left hand. He brought the bag to his nose and sniffed.

'Smells like something illegal to me. This yours, ain't it, Larry? This illegal dope here?'

Larry licked his lips. He glanced at Melanie, remembering what she'd said earlier about chain gangs and water moccasins.

'Man, what do you *want*?' he groaned again.

'You know what I want,' Lucas replied, implacable.

'Uh . . . OK. Yeah, sure. It's a deal.'

'*Say it*, you hippy piece of shit.'

Larry's voice had gone all quavery and soft, and he couldn't seem to stop licking his lips, or look Lucas in the face, either. He cleared his throat. 'Uh, yeah. You can have her. You can have the girl if you'll give me a ride.'

Lucas looked over at Mellie. 'How about it, girl? That deal OK with you, too?'

She stared at him in horror. The knife . . . poor Larry. What kind of madness was this? Her tongue moved almost without thought, and she blurted, 'Yes! Whatever you say, just don't hurt him!'

He held her terrified gaze for what seemed an eternity – and then he smiled. And with that it was over. Somehow Lucas's switchblade vanished as mysteriously as it had appeared, and an expression of pure sunshine transformed the hard lines of his face.

'Son, you got yourself a deal with this old peckerwood. Ben?'

'What's that, Lucas?'

'You been panting like a kid in a whorehouse to drive my car, well, now's your chance.' He flipped the keys and Ben snatched them from the air, one-handed, a grin of purest ecstasy stretching his jawbone out of shape.

'Wow, Lucas, I—'

'What you do is shut up and listen, Ben. You drive Larry here on up to the country line and let him out. Then you come on back here. I'll be waiting. And don't let anything happen to my car.'

'Oh, no, Lucas, I'll be real careful.'

'See that you do. Larry, climb on in there, take the shotgun. Been a real pleasure meeting you. Oh, Larry?'

'Huh?'

'Why don't you throw your duffel bag in first, and sit on that? I don't want you getting anything . . . nasty . . . on my upholstery. You dig?'

Larry climbed into the car and slammed the door, hard, to mask the destruction of something even he didn't quite recognize. Although Mellie, watching him as he carefully avoided looking at her, knew what it was.

Call it pride, self-image, plain and simple manhood, though Lucas had drawn not one drop of blood with his knife, he had cut that intangible *something* away from Larry as neat and clean as any surgeon.

She wondered if Larry would ever get it back. Looking at him, she kind of doubted it. Something about him looked . . . crippled to her now.

'Wahoo!' Ben let out a yell and tromped the pedal. The big GTO took off in a spinning cloud, the noise so loud that, a couple miles down the road, Larry was still trying to figure out if he'd really heard Lucas Buck holler, 'You have a nice life now, Mr Rosenweig.'

Chapter Four

'I suppose you're feeling proud of yourself right now?' Melanie said.

'Why, no, Melanie, I'm not. Not any more than I would if I stepped on some old termite gnawing a hole in my house. Just doing what needed to be done.'

Lucas raised one hand, palm up, and waggled his fingers in a come here motion. She noticed how long those fingers were, and wondered if the stories she'd heard about some kind of connection between finger length and . . .

She felt herself blush, then grow even hotter when Lucas grinned at her, slowly nodded his head up and down, and said, 'Yes, ma'am. It's true, too.'

He led her off the road to a chunk of deadwood in the shade of the oaks. Now that the sound of his car had diminished almost to nothing, only a thin, mosquito-like whine to mark whatever Ben was doing to it, other sounds began to intrude: the soft mumble of bees hanging above big purple balls of clover, a raucous, squawking crow flapping over-head, the nervous chitter of squirrels in the shadowy branches, and, shockingly loud, the long, low *maaaooooo*! of a nearby milker.

The air smelled of dry moss, fresh grass, newly turned soil. Early summer smells, unwilted by the terrific heat yet to come.

He dusted off a patch of the deadwood. 'Sit yourself down, Mellie Hankings, and tell me how you come to be running off with the likes of old Larry, there.'

She nodded. No matter what she thought of his methods, nobody had really gotten hurt, had they? And she wouldn't have bet even one dime on that outcome, the first time the big red Pontiac had blown on past and that dark brown beer bottle had come flying out of its slipstream as the car fishtailed wildly down the road. And this Lucas Buck – he sure did seem to live up to his reputation.

Which was, she asked herself, exactly what? Hand with the girls, that's all she could think of. Well, now she could see why, even plainer than that day last year at the ice cream social. Maybe it was because she was older. Or he was. Anyway, something was different now.

'Why was I leaving?' she said, unaware that she had already relegated the act to the past tense. 'Well, it all has to do with a redneck piece of trash name of Gage Temple . . .'

*　*　*

Ben dropped Larry Rosenweig off exactly ten feet past the Fulton County line. There wasn't much there, only more oaks on one side, a freshly ploughed field on the other, and bullet-pocked green country road signs facing in either direction.

'Here's where you get off, boy,' Ben said.

Larry tossed his duffel bag over the side, then kicked open the door.

'Hey, you be careful with this car. Lucas thinks a lot of it, and you don't want him knowing you hurt it none.'

Larry turned to face him. A twisted half-smile drew his thin lips out of shape. 'But you aren't Lucas, are you, Ben? That's your name, right? Ben?'

Nervously, Ben nodded. Larry raised his boot and deliberately slammed his heel as hard as he could into the side of the door. It made a hollow, plonking sound, and a round dent appeared.

'*Hey!*'

'I'm not planning to ever come back to this shit-heel place,' Larry snarled. 'But I want that Jew-hating redneck to have something to remember me by. And you, punk, if you want to climb out of that car, I'll give you something to remember, too.'

He advanced a step, and Ben suddenly noticed

that Larry, who had looked so small next to Lucas, wasn't really all that little at all. And he was at least two years older.

'You watch yourself, mister,' Ben said. 'You hurt his car, he'll come get your sorry ass.' Then he rammed the accelerator, swung the wheel hard left, and spun out. He'd hoped to get Larry with a good hard spray of roadside gravel, but no such luck. When he looked in the rear-view mirror, all he saw was Larry, standing by the road, right hand up, the single-finger salute steady as a rock until he finally vanished in the distance.

LeGage Temple, named after a forgotten general from the War of the Rebellion and called Gage by everybody who knew him, dug around in his right nostril for the booger that just wouldn't quite break loose. Finally he managed to hook the blackened tip of one untrimmed fingernail under the crusted scab and yank her right out of there.

'Got you, you bitch,' he said to nobody in particular. He looked up. 'Say, Marvis, you gonna hog that bottle of shine all to yourself? It's hot work, y'know, doin' this shade tree mechanic shit, especially when it ain't your own car. Know what I mean?'

Gage had both burly forearms propped on a drop cloth almost as blackened and greasy as the engine of the sixty-two Chevy pickup on which he was working. Marvis Pickney, a thin, sunken-chested man in his mid-twenties with a stubbled face that advertised several generations of poverty-induced malnutrition, spat a wad of milky-green looger in the same general direction as Gage had unloaded the contents of his right-hand nose hole.

'You get all shame-faced, Gage, you'll screw up something in my truck, now won't you? And if I could afford to take her to the Texaco and have her fixed right, I wouldn't be needing you in the first place.'

Gage stood away and slapped his greasy palms against the sides of his jeans. Dark hair curled at his wrists and exploded from the collar of his grimy T-shirt. The hair on his skull was thick and dark and relatively long – not from any urge towards the new-fangled hippy styles (Gage knew only one thing to do with hippy hair, and that involved a dull straight razor), but from a general lack of concern for any kind of formal grooming. Whenever his hair got long enough to get in the way of whatever he was doing, Gage took a big buck knife and hacked away until the problem disappeared. It was cheap and effective, and it suited his personality. Waste not, want not, his momma had always told him.

He wasn't exactly sure about all that. His momma hadn't wasted a damn thing her whole life, and his daddy hadn't either, but he couldn't ever remember anything but wanting. So maybe his momma had been mistaken. Sure as hell she wouldn't lie, though, and Gage would have killed anybody who would have suggested such a thing.

'Marvis, the day I can't do anything at all that needs doing on this piece of shit truck of yours, sober or knee-walking drunk, it don't matter, will be the day they lay me down in my coffin and close that hole for good. And speaking of holes, why don't you shut yours and toss that jug of shine over here?'

Sullenly, Marvis uncoiled himself from the split-log fence he'd been half leaning, half sitting on, and pitched the unmarked fruit jar of clear liquid over. Gage caught it one handed, lifted the wire retainer, and took a good swallow.

'Ah,' he said, holding the jar up to the light. 'M'maw put up a hell of a load of apple sauce and tomatoes and green beans and shit in these Globe canning jars. But I got to tell you, Marvis, if those Globe people never came up with any better use than moonshine for these bottles, far as I'm concerned, they already got their ticket straight for heaven.' He nodded to himself, raised the fruit jar, and bit off another good taste. Then he belched and tossed the jar back. 'That's real good,' he said.

Marvis moved a little way down the fence – the late afternoon sun was starting to slant in across Gage's barnyard and pop a few good ones right into Marvis's eyes – and watched as Gage dived back under the primer-coated hood.

After a time, he said, 'I seen you squiring that Hankings girl, Mellie, down to the movie theatre' – he pronounced it thee-*a*-ter – 'tuh other day. One of them monster shows, I think it was.'

'Oh, you did, did you? Well, maybe I did. And what of it?'

'Don't get your drawers in an uproar, Gage. I was just asking. What is she, about sixteen now?'

'Uh huh, about that.'

'Pretty little thing,' Marvis mused, rocking back on his heels.

Gage emerged from the engine compartment, a scowl on his broad features. He pulled a towel from his back pocket and began to wipe grease off his hands. 'Marvis, are you just flapping your jaw to hear the big bird sing, or are you trying to say something to me?'

'Huh? Say what to you, Gage? Was just asking, is all.'

'Well, to answer the question you're too goddamned dumb to ask, Marvis, yes. The answer is yes.' Gage reached into the side pocket of his biballs and pulled out a small, square box. Carefully, he flipped open the top. A tiny chip of diamond caught the light.

'Gonna pop the question to her this weekend, I think. She's only sixteen, but what the hell, with them Hankings women, that's ripe enough. She don't need no more schooling, neither, to be my wife. Knows how to cook and clean, and making babies comes with that package natural, I guess.'

Gage shrugged, folded up the ring box and put it away. 'Anyway, I do aim to ask her, probably on Friday. She said we could get together that night.' For a moment, Gage looked almost shy. 'I'm gonna take her to Carl's Rancho Steak House, do her up right.'

That nugget widened Marvis's eyes for sure. 'Jesus, Gage, that's the dearest joint in town. Set you back ten, fifteen bucks before you're done, bet you anything. All that money for little old Mellie Hankings – and a ring, too? Damn!'

'Well, shit, Marvis. What can I tell you? I love that girl.'

Christopher Buck shifted his broad rump uneasily, noticing every lump in the old pillow that cushioned the seat of his rocker. He had the rocker out on the back porch of his snug little parsonage, where he'd cut the eaten-out screen windows away years before to make it more open to the weather and the breezes.

He liked it better back here anyway. Sit out on the front porch, and you have to say hello to every Tom, Dick, and Jane that wanted to open your gate. Like visiting hours, almost. So when the soft time of the evening came around, the time when

Preacher Buck wanted his glass of sipping bourbon – Blanton's, usually, though he'd settle for Dickel in a pinch – he'd take the old rocker on the back porch every time.

Out there in the gloom – there was still a slow wash of red where the sun painted a final farewell across the western sky – the Preacher could see the remnants of blossoms. White and pink, what was left on the cherry trees, peach trees, and apple trees that filled his back yard. Out front of the house was his neatly trimmed lawn and his carefully kept petunia beds, but in back, away from the public eye, was something more untamed: the old orchard, some of the gnarled and leaning trees nearly wild now, and the ground beneath running with rambler roses, clumps of peonies where fat bees bumbled, and the odd oleander or two, filling the air with scent.

And beyond the yard, out there in the gathering dark on the far side of the rusted out post-and-bobwire fence, the graveyard. Old place, real old. Nobody used it any more, hadn't for maybe thirty years, although the Reverend Buck thought that when his time came, he might like to lay down in the tangled silence there.

From here he couldn't see the gravestones, but in his mind's eye they were plain enough. Old, flaking, grey, tilted one way or another like bad teeth in a rotten mouth, their surfaces nearly scraped clean of any meaning. Dumb and empty, marking things so old no living mind held any recollection of them.

It was said there had been burying done here long before the white man came, that either the Catawba or the Tuscarora tribes had laid their shamans to rest in that ancient spot out beyond his fruit trees.

He rocked and sipped and thought about all that. Nothing there to doubt, really. He knew all he needed to know about that graveyard. It had been his doing that the old families no longer used it. Back when he'd first been ordained, it had come to him that it was time to close that book, at least for reading in public. Let the dead rest there undisturbed, whether white man or Indian. He still called them Indians, or even injuns, in the privacy of his mind, though they'd been Native Americans in his sermons for at least ten years now.

He grunted softly as he stared at the backs of his big hands. In the thick, creamy shadows of evening, the veins stood out in great black ridges, and he fancied his skin had grown so thin he could make out the pulse of his own blood.

There'd been a time, it seemed like just last week, or maybe last month, when the skin there had been smooth and unmarked, and the veins hidden, just as the strength of those hands – strangler's hands, some said – had always been hidden.

He raised his heavy cut-glass tumbler and let

another taste of the Blanton's slide down his throat, a dollop of liquid fire to feed the warm glow in his belly.

Lucas. What to do about Lucas? He knew the question was not entirely his own. Part of it came from the darkness out there, from the things hidden in the yawning earth beyond his orchard. Let the dead rest? Well, some folks might be surprised to know just how lively the dead could get, especially in Trinity. Especially in Preacher Buck's graveyard.

He could feel them press against his thoughts, like great dark invisible moths, wings shimmering with slime, smelling of stagnant water and sour, worm-roiled earth. They'd been there as long as he could remember. Sometimes, when he thought about the future—

But no. No time for that yet. He might weigh fifty pounds more than he had as a young man, might have a bit of trouble fitting his big old rear into the rocking chair these days, might even find himself wheezing and his heart rapping like a fire-house bell after just climbing his own front steps, but he had a few years yet. Which was a good thing, because he wasn't at all sure about Lucas, not sure at all. One thing was true; his boy was the strongest Buck to come along in two hundred years, maybe the strongest one of all. That made him immensely valuable, but it also made him questionable; Preacher Buck knew that pure power, in and of itself, acknowledged no master by right, only by the force of a greater power. The graveyard would have to fight for his son, if it wanted him for its own.

The shadows in the graveyard seemed suddenly to gather in, and the air grew dark and thick around the Preacher's back porch. For just a moment, he sniffed a faint odour of burning sulphur. But then it passed, and the evening breeze was clear again.

Preacher Buck raised his glass for a final sip. Damned doctors, only let him have two a day now, said it might even be healthy. He'd long ago given up the ropy green cigars he used to walk out from the big house to the end of the orchard to smoke, lest his wife catch him out. She never could abide cigars, rest her soul.

He chuckled at the obvious omission. Not *God* rest her soul. Christopher Buck couldn't ever remember believing in any God. And when Hester had left this vale of tears, though everybody thought she was resting in sweet repose over at the big public cemetery, if she was resting in peace at all, it was out there in the dark, on the other side of the bobwire.

He knew. He'd dug her up and moved her himself, one cold and windy October night.

Which didn't mean spit, nowadays. What to do about Lucas, though. That was a real problem.

He would have to think on it for a while.

*   *   *

'Now let me get this straight,' Lucas said. 'You heard from old lady Rice, whose husband runs the jewelry store, that Gage was in there buying you an engagement ring? He ever mention anything like that to you before?'

Melanie sighed. She was sitting in a low crouch, the deadwood stump only lifting her a few inches above the low grass, so that her chin rested on her knees, and she had her arms wrapped around her shins. Lucas thought she looked like some kind of wildflower, caught there in the grass with the rest of the daisies and clover and Queen Anne's lace.

'Well, he didn't exactly mention it, but I could see it coming. Can't say that when Miz Rice told me it was any big surprise.'

Lucas was squatting, balanced on the balls of his feet, forearms resting across the top of his thighs, right on the edge of the pavement in the circle of shade from the oaks. Overhead the sun had tipped over towards evening, and the super-heated paleness had gone out of the sky. Already, far to the east, a band of purple was slowly leaking up to tint the fading horizon. The evening breeze, now sweet and cool, carried with it the dark fragrance of slow water drifting and the distant cries of kids at swimming holes along the river.

'So how do you feel about all that? Can't say I

know Gage all that well, but he seems like a nice enough fellow.'

'Oh, he's a nice fellow, all right. And that's all he is. Lucas, nobody ever accused Gage Temple of being at the front of the line when God handed out brains.'

Lucas grinned faintly. 'Well, Mellie, to tell you the truth, nobody ever said that about the Hankings folks, either.'

And though it surprised her, she felt the sting of that one, although she'd heard it a thousand times before. But this time it brought her to her feet. 'You listen to me, Lucas Buck. You can't judge every book by its cover.'

But he was already shaking his head, both hands up, palms out. He stood. 'Hey, hold on there, Mellie. Wasn't saying anything about you. But you got to admit, not very many folks would find anything strange at all about you and Gage getting hitched. Except he might be a shade old, but hell, what is it? Ten years? Even that's not much out of the ordinary. We're still country people, out here in the boondocks.'

She came up close to him, and suddenly he found himself intensely aware of her small, hard breasts beneath her T-shirt. She didn't press against him, but he knew she was very close to it. There was a dangerous green glint in her eyes, too.

'Lucas, my sister married out of the usual way for Hankings girls, and I ain't gonna throw my life

68

away on some stump puller like Gage Temple, no matter how nice he is.'

'I see. So you were going to – what? Hitch yourself up to something like Larry?'

'Oh, hell, Lucas. I didn't plan to marry him. But I figured if I had to run to get away from whatever Gage thinks is already written down on stone, I might as well find somebody who knew a little something about where I was planning to go. Larry was handy, is all.'

Lucas stared down at her, something dark caught like an insect in the precise centre of his gaze, and after a moment she felt it boring in on her, and she stepped back. 'Not that it's any business of yours anyhow,' she said at last.

'No, Mellie, it isn't. Well, it wasn't before today, but I tell you what. I don't want you to worry about Gage Temple any more. You understand me? Old Gage, he's a thing of the past. You just let Lucas Buck do your worrying for you – it's a hell of a lot easier on everybody concerned, I guarantee it. Is it a deal?'

Then he reached out one of his big hands to her. 'How about it, Mellie? Shake on it?'

She nodded slowly, as she heard the GTO winding down the distant miles, rushing closer. Her fingers closed on his with a slight, electric tingle.

'If you say so, Lucas,' she told him. 'Deal.'

But she wasn't sure.

Maybe there would be trouble.

Chapter Five

Lucas seemed preoccupied, as far as Ben could tell when he came back and picked up him and Mellie Hankings. They were both standing at the side of the road, spectral in the sweet-smelling dusk, when he pulled up next to them.

'Lucas, that boy kicked a dent in your door. I'm sorry, I couldn't stop him. He did it before I even knew what he was up to.'

Inside, Ben was deeply worried. This was the first time Lucas had entrusted the GTO into his care, and he'd let some Yankee snotnose half kick a hole in it. He wouldn't blame Lucas if he never gave him another chance. Or even if he just dragged him out onto the roadside and pounded on his bootie for a while.

But Lucas handed Mellie into the front bucket seat and said, 'I got eyes, Ben. Now, why don't you shinny into the back seat there and hold your water. I'll attend to Larry when I get around to it.'

This was so far beyond what Ben had expected,

riding back down that darkening highway with a head full of nameless fear, that the relief of it was palpable. He felt a distinct loosening of the muscles around his chest and gut, and had to stifle a sudden urge to pee – although that could have been nothing more than the Pearl beer.

And so he climbed into the back seat, next to the grocery sack full of Pearl bottles, mostly empty, and rooted around till he found a full one. 'You want some of this beer, Lucas?'

Lucas shook his head.

'Mellie?'

'Thanks kindly, Ben, but no thanks.'

A tenuous kind of silence descended, not a real one, for Lucas cranked the car off with his usual style, and that overbored block and those glass-paks made their usual racket. But a silence nonetheless, one that, if Ben had possessed just a little more *depth* than he did, he might have called spiritual. A pocket of soul-deep quiet, just ghosting along with the car like an invisible bubble with them inside.

They came up on the river bridge at a good clip, and Ben called out, 'Hold up there, Lucas. Let's get rid of this mess.'

Lucas pulled over and Ben climbed out with the sack of empties, peered over the railing at the brown-green water sliding below like cool molasses, then heaved the sack over. It made a single loud splash and then was gone.

'You didn't kill no kids on that raft by the bridge, did you, Ben?' Lucas asked.

'Nobody there, Lucas. All gone home, I guess.' He sighed, and glanced up at the sky. Blue-black up there, soft, and already full of quiet stars. For one moment Ben was very glad he was just a country boy, though he knew that didn't cut much ice in the more important places. But since his place was here, and would always be so, he didn't worry about it.

'Nice,' he murmured as he got back in the car.

'It is that,' Lucas replied, and off they went.

'That you, Gage Temple?'

Gage shifted himself a little, sitting on the top step of the front porch of his big old tumbledown farmhouse. Willow the wisps floated off in the young hayfields out front, and whippoorwills cried in the night. Somewhere off in the distance, gulls wandered inland from the sea, their calls as lonesome as the stars up above.

'I see you, Lucas Buck. What brings you out in the night? You got car troubles again? I told you those glasspaks weren't heavy enough for that bored-out block.'

Lucas drifted in closer, stepped up, and set himself down next to Gage. The boards of the step creaked softly as they took his weight. He had a bottle of Black Daniels by the neck.

'Thought I'd bring you a taste of something besides that shine you're always drinking, Gage.'

'Why, Lucas, that's nice of you. Ain't nothing wrong with the goat, then?'

Lucas shook his head. He handed the bottle over, watched Gage tilt it up and hold it, his Adam's apple jigging like a cork in a waterfall.

'Whoa, there, boy. Leave a little for me.'

Gage lowered the bottle, belched once, and handed it back. 'Fine whiskey,' he offered.

Lucas wiped the neck of the bottle in the crook of his shirtsleeve and poured a good swallow down his own throat. The two men sat then, silent, caught in the greater silence of the dark. Finally Lucas exhaled softly. 'Hear you got a thing going with the younger Hankings girl.'

Gage slapped the top of one thigh with a country-ham fist. 'Now, that goddamned Marvis got a mouth on him like a hound at the hunt, don't he? One of these days I'm gonna waltz him round back of the barn and whip him till he screams like a woman.'

'Hey, Gage, it's no secret.'

Gage coughed up a bit of phlegm and spat viciously. 'Supposed to be. But you're right, it ain't. Everybody seems to know about it. Well, so what if I do? You got any reason to stick your oar in?'

'Whoa, calm down, Gage. Here, have another snort. I'm just talking.' He pushed the bottle at

Gage until he took it again. Gage's second snort was at least as healthy as his first, and Lucas nodded approval.

'Nice to see a man enjoy his liquor. Some say it isn't any good for you, but real men know the truth, now don't they, Gage?'

'Bible-shouting pussy wipes is all they are, Lucas. Whiskey was good enough for my pap, and his pappy too. Reckon it'll do me fine, just like them.'

Lucas nodded thoughtfully, recalling that Gage's granddaddy had died at the age of forty-seven, falling off his tractor into the hay baler, drunk as a mule. And Gage's mama had walked around Trinity for years, talking about tripping down steps, walking into doors, slipping in mud puddles. Most of those injuries occurred of a weekend, Fridays or Saturdays when the Blue Wren ran its happy hour specials that her husband favoured so much, so that she almost always wore an old-fashioned black hat with a heavy black veil to church on Sundays. This went on till Carver Temple, Gage's daddy, had a little summertime accident of his own, driving his beat-up Plymouth into the abutment of the C&O overpass a mile down from the Blue Wren at eighty miles an hour on a soft Friday evening. Taken all together, the Temple men tended to have a lousy life expectancy, but since they seldom bought life insurance, it wasn't much of a concern.

Oddly enough, Roberta Temple seemed to miss the wife-beating sonofabitch, for over the next year she shrank in on herself, until finally she shrivelled all the way up and died. Doctors called it cancer, but Lucas thought it was something even more certainly fatal than the black tumour stick. Love, probably.

'Well, the reason I mentioned it was I happened to see Mellie today.'

Gage turned slightly, his feelers quivering now. 'You did? Where'd you see her? I didn't even know you knew her to talk to.'

'Well, Gage, I didn't, but when I run across her two miles beyond the river bridge, hitchhiking north with the ugliest hippy Jew boy you ever did see, I figured I'd better stop and make my acquaintance.'

Both of Gage's black, grease-soaked clod-hoppers hit the bottom of the steps at the same time with a crack that startled a couple of crows roosting in the eaves. They flapped out in a chorus of rasping crow-shouts.

'What's that you're telling me?'

'Now, hold on, Gage. I took care of it for you. Ran that hippy boy clean out of Fulton County, and brought old Mellie back, safe as a tick in a dog's ear.'

Gage clamped fingers like a set of pipe wrenches around Lucas's wrist. 'Where is she?' he whispered hoarsely. 'What'd you do with her?'

Lucas didn't say anything. He looked down at his wrist, up into Gage's red-shot eyes, and back down again. And waited.

After a long moment, Gage said, 'Uh. I'm . . . sorry, Lucas.' He let go. 'Got a little carried away there, you understand.'

'Why, sure I do, Gage. Worried about that girl of yours. And there isn't a thing for you to worry about. I took her right home and dropped her off.'

Gage thought about it. 'Lucas?'

'Hm?'

'She say anything? You know. About . . . why?'

Lucas waited a few beats, then said, 'Well, Gage, I expect that's something you ought to talk to her about. You know, private. I said I wasn't gonna stick my oar in.'

Suddenly Gage rose to his feet, an agonized expression on his blunt features. He turned and slammed one fist as hard as he could into the porch pillar at the top of the steps, hit it so hard the whole porch roof shivered.

'God *damn* it! She never said nothing at all to me.'

'Well, I don't know what it's all about either, Gage, but I do know one thing.'

'What's that, Lucas?'

'Well, if it weren't for me, you wouldn't have any chance at all of finding out what's what, now would you? I mean, if I hadn't come along when I did, she'd be halfway to New York City with that hippy by now. And you with nothing but that diamond ring in your pocket there to remember her by.'

Involuntarily, Gage's hand brushed the side of his biballs. He stared down at Lucas, the greasy skin of his face pouchy with misery. 'I'm gonna talk to her,' he said.

'You do that. But remember who made things so you could. Right?'

Gage nodded. 'Fair's fair, Lucas. I owe you one. That's a true deal.'

Lucas stood up, dusted off the seat of his jeans, and stretched. Overhead, the moon had just set sail across its starry course, fat and round as a fresh peach.

'Deal,' Lucas answered, and slapped Gage hard on the shoulder. 'Maybe someday you can do me a little favour.' And he drifted off into the night, silky as a ghost.

Gage stood, looking down at his clodhoppers as if he'd never seen shoes before, till he heard the throttled roar of the GTO making its way out of his lane.

He sat back down and picked up the bottle of Black Daniels Lucas had left behind. It was empty.

'Damn,' Gage said.

Hepzibah Hankings, called Heppy by the few women friends her husband, Joshua, allowed her to keep, turned a gaze of pure brown flint on her daughter as she closed the front door behind her.

'Where you been, girl?'

'Hi, Ma. How are you?'

'Don't you show me your mouth, now. I'll slap it right off your face. The Lord says—'

'Ma, I'm sorry. I'm tired. And I know the Lord don't like me much. Is there anything left from supper?'

Heppy Hankings took the ends of her apron, lifted it off her lap, covered her face with it for a moment, then laid it back down. It was a gesture Mellie knew well – down at the Resurrection Revival Church, it was meant as a sign of submission to the will of the Lord. You saw a lot of it when they were passing the big rattlesnakes and water moccasins back and forth, down in front of the altar.

'I wrapped a plate up for you in tin foil. It's on the top shelf of the Frigidaire. Your daddy said I ought to throw it to the pigs, teach you a lesson, but . . .' She shook her head. 'But we ain't got no pigs.'

And for a moment her thin, tired face looked so desolate that Mellie thought her heart would permanently crack. 'Oh, Mama, I really am sorry. I got all wound up with something, and I just clean forgot about the time.'

She knew she would burn in hell for lying to her mother, of all people, but she'd come to realize, as she got older, that hell might be a bit closer than some fiery place down at the end of the road. There were times, she felt, that hell was right here, inside this town, even inside this very house. But she said nothing of that, just knelt by her mother on the rump-sprung sofa and put her arms around those frail shoulders.

After a time, Heppy sniffed, then slid an appraising look in her daughter's direction. 'You over at Gage Temple's place, were you?'

'Huh? What makes you say that?'

'Nothing makes me say it. I'm your mother, though. Got eyes in my head, too. That man's fixing to marry you, mark my words. And I don't think you're so empty-headed you don't know it yourself.'

'Mama, Gage isn't fixing to marry me. Don't know if I'd have him anyhow.'

'Mellie, he's an honest man. Maybe drinks a little, like all them Temples, but he'll take care of you. Man's good with his hands like that, his wife won't never have to worry where the groceries is coming from.'

'Mama, I am *not* going to marry Gage Temple.'

'Who, then?' her mother asked simply. 'Lucas Buck?'

'Now that,' Preacher Buck said, 'was a fine leg of lamb, Marie.'

Lucas Buck, sitting across from him, nodded agreement. 'Sure was, Marie. Don't know how you do it.'

The inside of the parsonage was bigger than it looked; there was a parlour along the front of the house with a large bay window overlooking the porch, and behind it a small kitchen that opened into the dining room and a hallway, a bathroom, and two bedrooms, the smaller of which the Reverend used for a den and office. Living alone, he spent most of his time in this room, venturing into the parlour only on formal occasions to entertain the few guests he was willing to receive in the parsonage itself.

Marie, huge and old, her broad shoulders now showing the hump of age, perpetually draped in black lace with her white hair pinned in a bun at the back of her neck, came in five days a week to keep house for him. The church paid her, though she would probably have done it for free. She'd been a good friend to Hester Buck, before Hester had so unfortunately passed on, and she'd come on over to the parsonage when the Preacher had abandoned the big house for good. Not the least of her charms was that she never put any stock in the ugly rumours about the Preacher and Hester and that night Hester passed over into the hands of the Lord.

She stuck her head past the swinging door to the kitchen, a cloud of steam billowing out around her, and wisps of white hair floating across her flat, oddly unlined face. 'Thank you kindly, boys. Always does a body good, Lucas, to see the way you can tuck my cooking in. And you, Reverend.' She uttered a short chuckle. 'You been doing the same thing for a lot longer than your boy, I guess. No surprises there.'

She vanished then, the door swinging behind her, a genie popped back into her culinary bottle.

'Yeah, Daddy, you tuck Marie's cooking in just fine. Can see it from here.'

Lucas's everlasting snottiness irritated the Preacher, but it wasn't a new thing, and the superb meal he'd just finished – except for a pie made from the last of the winter apples, whose tantalizing cinnamon odour was sinking grappling hooks deep into his mental taste buds as he sat there waiting for it – all of it came together to put him in an unaccustomed expansive mood.

'Lucas, been meaning to have a little talk with you.'

Lucas shoved his chair back a bit from the oak table and its spotless white cloth – another reason Marie was a pearl beyond price was her skills on laundry day – and splayed his legs out as he tipped his chair back on its hind legs.

'Know you have, Daddy. I've been wondering when you'd get around to spitting it out.'

The Preacher cocked his big head to the side, his

midnight sapphire eyes wide and innocent – and hard as the stones they mimicked.

'Think you know everything, Lucas, do you?'

Lucas folded his hands across his lean belly and yawned. 'I know enough, Daddy. But I bet you've got a load more for me, haven't you? How about we quit dancing around the maypole and get down to the nut squeezing?'

Preacher Buck propped his elbows on the table-cloth, put his palms together and steepled them beneath his many chins and said, 'Have you given any thought to your future, Lucas?'

'What about my future, Daddy?'

Preacher Buck moved his big shoulders dis-missively. 'Lucas, I know you think this cat and mouse game of yours is cute, but I just don't see the charm of it. You know damned well what I'm talking about. The responsibilities we Buck men have to carry. Have always carried. Our . . . duties, if you will, to the town of Trinity.'

'Well, now, that sure is a pretty way of putting it. Duties. Responsibilities. Why don't you just come out and say it, Daddy? It isn't as if I'm blind. Or that I've never wandered around that rotting old graveyard by the light of a full moon.'

The Preacher peered over his fingertips at Lucas for what seemed a long time. Long enough that in the sight of Lucas's mind, his father's eyes glazed over, lost their living sheen, and became blank and blue as the eyes of a doll. An old, ugly, scary doll with a swollen potato nose scarred by red bourbon veins and teeth like yellow tombstones behind lips sheened the colour of wet chicken skin. A wind came up and rattled the shutters of the house, like an insistent crone demanding entrance.

Lucas grinned. 'And you can cut the sound effects, too, Daddy. They don't scare me at all.'

Preacher Buck blinked, and the life came back into him. 'Why, Lucas. What are you talking about, boy? I'm not trying to scare you. Last thing on my mind. But we do have to talk about the future. Your future, mine, the town.'

Lucas lifted both his arms and stretched like a cat. 'Well, Daddy, if what history I know is anything close to right, the minute my future starts will be the same minute yours ends. And the town will go on just like it always has, for all these years and years.'

'Now, Lucas, I'm not talking about the . . . ultimate . . . end. Not yet, not by a long shot. I'm not ready for anything like that, and neither are you.'

Suddenly Preacher Buck leaned forward, and this time his eyes glowed in his face. Once again the wind came up, and a stray gust flickered across the candles in the middle of the table, casting long, strange shadows across the Preacher's face.

'Unless you think you're ready now . . . Lucas? Do you? Do you think you're ready?'

Lucas found himself drawn forward by the preternatural power of that gaze, felt himself begin to sink into its dark-blue depth, and only after a concentrated effort of will was he able to tear himself away from it.

Even so, the experience left him shaken, and he felt a sheen of cold sweat on his brow and in his armpits. 'Daddy,' he said carefully. 'You know I hope you stick around this vale of tears until you are good and ready to shuffle off. Whenever the hell that is, and damn well your own choice.'

The candles flared up again as Preacher Buck sank back, beads of sweat glittering on his own corpulent cheeks. Both men knew something had just been decided, tests made and passed or failed, and a groundwork built which might serve well enough for future negotiations.

Preacher Buck nodded. 'Well, thank you, Lucas. A son's devotion to his father is always a fine thing to see.'

Marie bustled in just then, juggling two large white plates of steaming apple pie. 'I put the American cheese on it, Reverend, just the way you like it. Lucas, you want some?'

He showed his white teeth in a saturnine grin. 'You bet, ma'am. Nobody bakes apple pie like you.'

*   *   *

Gage Temple was driving the old Plymouth his daddy had killed himself in. It had taken him two years of concentrated labour to put the old beater back together, since he had to hit just about every junkyard on the Carolina coasts at one time or another, looking for spare parts.

He couldn't explain, even to himself, why he'd done such a crazy thing, but the car was a comfort to him. Not to mention that when he finished with it, it was in one hell of a lot better shape than it had been since it came off the showroom floor new, back in 1982.

He was driving it now, cruising up and down Oleander Drive, back and forth in front of the Rice Jewelry Store, trying to make up his mind. He'd been doing this for almost two hours, even pulling in a couple of times to one of the slant-painted reserved parking slots in front of the store. But he pulled back out both times, because whenever he took out the ring box and then tried to climb out of the Plymouth, his nerve failed him. Well, not his nerve. Not exactly.

He knew what it was. He just wasn't ready to give up. Not yet.

That little ring had cost him two hundred dollars. Of course he had nothing like that laying around in fruit jar cash, buried out in the back yard, and so he signed up for one of the Rice Jewelry's E-Z Payment Plans, where he paid ten dollars a month for the rest of his life, seemed like.

But he didn't care, not when he did it, because he thought Melanie Hankings would like the ring, and even more, like what it represented. The sacrifice it meant, that he was willing to mortgage himself and his labour for a very long time in order to put the diamond, which the TV said was the symbol of eternal love – a diamond is forever, and he believed that – on her left hand ring finger.

Not many Temple women had ever gotten such a thing from their men, a real diamond to wear. So it *meant* something to him, and taking it back to the jewelry store meant something as well; that he was admitting it was over and, worst of all, over before it had really started.

He fished the old brass railroad repeater he'd gotten from his pap out of the kangaroo pocket of his biballs and checked the time. Ten minutes till five. Rice's would close up promptly at five. He watched the storefront float past. The slanting afternoon light slipped beneath its striped green-and-white awning to catch on the watches and rings and pieces of cheap silver plate arrayed there, then snapped back through the glass in unexpected sparkles.

He folded up the watch and put it back in his biballs, downshifted to second, and gentled the accelerator down. He took the corner at a smooth twenty-five miles an hour. Tomorrow was Friday. She'd said she would see him then. He now knew she'd never planned to keep that date, but she was still here.

He'd know more tomorrow, he told himself.

'Daddy, I take care of my own, just like you do. I been doing it for years. Thought you knew all about it.'

They were out on the back porch, a jug of Blanton's on the table between them, Preacher Buck rocking slowly, Lucas sitting spraddle-legged on an old kitchen chair turned backwards. The scent of faded blossoms filled the still evening air. Overhead, the evening star twinkled bright as wishes.

'Lucas, I knew you were out there, doing whatever it was you were doing. But I can't say our paths crossed all that much. And when they did, I just turned my face away, 'cause I didn't want to interfere. Some things, I figured, you had to learn for yourself. Same way I learned them, the school of hard knocks, boy.'

Lucas gazed off down the orchard, trying to make out shapes in the murk beyond, but with no luck, not even with that fat moon riding overhead, so sharp and ivory clear it looked like the very top of a perfectly bleached skull.

'So what, exactly, of my business did you run across, Daddy?'

'Well, I know you loaned Gage Temple some

money to pay off the mortgage on his daddy's farm after old Carver pancaked himself on the railroad crossing. And I knew you got that money from an account you started down to the First Merchant's Bank back in second grade, when you was selling protection from devils to the kids in your class for a quarter a week. Funny how all them quarters add up, isn't it?'

Lucas smiled faintly. 'The magic of compound interest, Daddy. And I suppose there's no use asking how you know about my bank accounts, is there? I thought I found the one bank in town you didn't own a piece of.'

Preacher Buck chuckled softly. 'Lucas, there isn't no such thing as a bank like that. Not in Trinity. I inherited a lot of what I got, and built on it like every Buck has. And someday you'll get it all, just like I did. But I think you'll have put together your own pile pretty good by that time.'

'Daddy, I already have. Not everything is here in Fulton County, you know. There's banks up in Wilmington, even in Baltimore and New York City.'

'New York City?' the Preacher replied, stretching it out like the TV commercial for the hot pepper sauce. They both laughed at that.

The Preacher's laughter trailed off in an unhealthy liquid gurgle, and he took a quick sip of his bourbon. 'You making good deals, Lucas?'

Lucas nodded. 'It's in the blood, Daddy. All us Bucks make good deals, seems like.'

'But you're not ready yet, are you?'

Lucas stared into the darkness beyond the rusty back fence. 'No, Daddy, I'm not ready. Not yet.'

Chapter Six

Melanie had put on her best summer frock, a jazzy thing she'd bought from the Sears and Roebuck downtown, with a halter top and bows and a flaring light blue skirt, to wear to Chrissy's house for lunch on Friday.

'I only got the one hour, Mellie, and you know Peter will gripe about that anyway, but you're my only baby sister, so you come right on over.' That's what Christine told her on the phone, after a pause just barely long enough to let her know that though it was a small sacrifice, it was still a sacrifice, and that while blood was blood, changed circumstances had carved a gap.

Now they sat in the kitchen of the old Victorian house Peter had bought with part of the money he got from selling his daddy's three crabbing boats. This was the only part of the house Christine had got around to remodelling, but Melanie loved what she had done here: fine new light-coloured oak cabinets, a built-in Maytag dishwasher, two sinks, each with its own disposal unit, a range sunk right into the counter top with both an oven and a broiler mounted above, and a refrigerator with two doors, one for a freezer, and an ice cube machine in there, too.

Over by the back door, which stood open to the aluminum screen door that led to the back porch, was a breakfast nook Chrissy had re-upholstered in shiny red vinyl – the kind with little silver sparkles in it. Sitting there brought back ghostly intimations of the red bucket seats in Lucas Buck's Pontiac convertible, and reminded Mellie once again why she had come.

'These are real pretty napkins, Chrissy. Where'd you get them?'

Christine Emory was eleven years older than her sister, taller, darker, and heavier, though with the same determined cast to her strong features. The approach to thirty and the front gate to middle age had been kind to her. Like Melanie, she had never met the conventional southern standards for beauty – there was too much force and not enough yield in her looks for that – but as she'd aged, everybody agreed she'd become another desirable southern standard: a right handsome woman.

She was not entirely unaware of this, though she tried not to let it influence her thinking, especially when it came to the storm clouds she could dimly make out on the very private horizon she shared with her husband Peter. And she might have liked to discuss those turbulent weathers with her baby sister, if it hadn't been that Peter Emory was the only decent catch a Hankings woman had made in four or five generations, and so she wasn't ready to tarnish that with talk about how things might not be turning out quite as perfectly as she'd once hoped. Besides, from the looks of things, it wasn't her big sis's problems Mellie had come here to talk about.

'Sent off to a store in Indianapolis for them. L. S. Ayers, I think it was. I got the catalogue around here somewhere, if you want.'

Dreamily, Mellie shook her head as she ran her fingertips across the cheerful flowered fabric. 'Indiana . . . Larry was from around there someplace. Not Indianapolis, I don't think.'

'Larry? Who's this Larry, sissy? Here, have a little more of this salad. Fresh crab sure is good, isn't it?'

So Mellie told Christine all about Larry Whatsisname, and Gage Temple, and Lucas Buck.

'I guess I don't know what to do, Chrissy. Somebody seen me riding around in the Buckmobile and got right on the party line to Mama, so of course she knew all about it before I even got home. Well, not all, but enough to let me know she doesn't have any use for Lucas Buck. Which means the little birds have probably been singing in Gage's ear, too, just like they did in mine about that damned ring he bought me.'

'You want some more of this two per cent, sissy? I got a fresh carton in the refrigerator over there.'

Mellie sighed. 'I love to listen to you talk, Chrissy. I was only ten or so when you married Peter, so I guess I didn't notice things as much. But I bet you're the first woman in our family ever to talk about refrigerators instead of fridges or iceboxes. And you probably don't even think about what you're saying.'

Christine Emory stared at her little sister for a long time after she said that, for it was exactly true, and it hit the mark harder than Melanie could have imagined.

Chrissy *didn't* think about it anymore, though at one time it was all she did think about: how to walk, and talk, and the right fork to use, and how to set a table, and all the things the quality girls took for granted, because they just absorbed them through their skin as they grew up. But for her, each and every trinket of knowledge or habit, even the smallest – like refrigerator instead of fridge – had been gained only through the hardest of labour.

And now she took it for granted, so much so that it took this off-handed observation from little Melanie to bring home with shocking force just how far she'd come, and how far her younger sister wanted to go.

'Oh, Mellie,' she whispered, 'if you don't want to

marry Gage Temple, I'll help you. You just tell me what you want.'

And she thought, *Yes, anybody but Gage Temple.*

Melanie lowered her eyes. 'Lucas Buck tells me not to worry about Gage. He says we've got a deal between us, and for me not to worry, that as far as I'm concerned, Gage is a thing of the past.'

But Christine had heard a few things about Lucas Buck and his deals, and so she tilted her head to one side and said, 'You watch yourself around that Buck boy, Mellie. He's a slick one, and I'm not sure he's up to everything he ought to be.' She tapped one strong finger absently on the edge of the table. Maybe things would work out OK, after all.

'Still, Lucas Buck is quality,' she said at last. 'There's no getting around that . . .'

'Hello, Gage.'

'Mellie. Ma'am, Josh.' Gage wore a rumpled, shapeless John Deere tractor cap, which he tipped in the direction of Melanie's parents, who were seated in the living room. Heppy had her knitting in her lap and her reading glasses – not eye doctor prescription, just the plastic kind you could buy at Walgreens – tipped up in her salt and pepper hair. Josh sat on a recliner chair covered in dark purple fake leather, all creased and sweat-stained where his hands, head and butt had put permanent black marks. He had it cranked back so his feet were up and he was almost invisible behind the barrier of the *Trinity Guardian* he had folded open across his chest. He rattled the pages and said, 'Gage, how do.'

'Come to take Mellie out for a spell,' Gage mumbled.

'Oh, come on, Gage,' Melanie said. 'Let's just go.' She pushed past him and slipped out. He turned, just in time to catch the screen door swinging shut on his face.

'Ouch.'

'Boy, you sure are a clumsy one, ain't you?' Josh chuckled.

Gage flushed a dull brick-red, mumbled something indistinguishable, turned, and made his retreat to the small front porch. Melanie stood there next to the top of the double step that went down to the walk. Her mother kept on planting marigolds along the walk, to keep off the bugs, she said, but they always died. They were still alive now, but not for long, Melanie judged.

'Well, uh. You come on, then, Mellie.'

'I don't know, Gage.'

'What?'

'You heard me. I don't know if I want to go with you.'

He hadn't planned on things taking a turn like this. Or, rather, the idea of it had crossed his mind, but the possibility was so awful he had simply ignored it, that she wouldn't want to talk to him at all. For a moment he just stood there, his mouth slowly opening and closing like a catfish dragged out of the water and left to dry in the sun.

'Come on, Mellie,' he got out finally. 'Why you doing this to me? I ain't never tried to hurt you. Come on, let's get off this porch and go somewhere we can talk. Please?'

She stepped forward, stopped, then nodded. 'Okay, we do have to talk, I guess. And this sure ain't the place for it. So all right, let's go. You drove that Plymouth of yours, didn't you?'

'Uh huh.'

'Good. Let's go out by the river bridge. It ought to be private enough out there somewhere.'

The cast-iron engine block of the GTO was built to take a lot of pressure, and what Lucas had done to it made it even more of a racing machine, but at the moment it was purring soft as a baby kitten as Lucas cruised slowly through the darkened streets of downtown.

Here and there he passed other cars, most of them full of kids younger than him, even a few pickups with boys in from the country, five or six of them piled up in the truck beds with a case of Pearl or Dixie to split amongst themselves. They wore their hair mostly in crew cuts or flat tops or straight buzz cuts – even now, five or six years into the new age, the hippy styles hadn't made much of an inroad among the farm boys of South Carolina. Or the city boys, either, Lucas thought, as he raked his fingers through his own hair, which hung dangerously over his ears and curled almost to his shirt collar.

Oddly enough, nobody had ever called Lucas out about his hair.

He was thinking about this when he drove out from under a dense patch of sycamores and a shaft of moonbeam bounced off the hood of his car, turning the blood-red paint magically black in the bleached light of the moon.

Lucas glanced up, a puzzled expression on his face, as if he'd forgotten something. He reached out and turned down the radio, whose tinny speaker was blatting something out of a Baltimore station . . . Do-wah-dittie, dittie dum dittie doo . . .

Hot guitars. Dittie *dum*.

'Got it,' he murmured, and ran the stop sign at the next corner as he turned back around the block. He'd been heading in exactly the wrong direction, if he wanted to go out by the river bridge . . .

Just before the river bridge was a single lane dirt road that turned off to the right and meandered down along the river bank a half mile or so, before dead-ending in a spot frequented by fishermen during the day, and kids looking for a bit of sweaty privacy at night.

Gage steered the Plymouth to one side of this dusty patch and turned off the engine. They sat for a minute, listening to the tick of the car as it settled. Then Gage heaved a sigh, opened his door and climbed out. He wandered aimlessly over to a ring of seared, blackened rock that showed the marks of a hundred campfires. Empty beer bottles glittered in shoals and – he averted his eyes – scumbags draped limply here and there, pale in the dark like the shed skins of mysterious snakes. He squatted and aimlessly stirred the ashes with one lumpy forefinger.

'Gage?'

'What's that, Mellie?'

She came up behind him, glanced down at his hulking, shadowy form, then walked past him and down to the bank of the river. It was rocky here, where the current had eaten out the soft bank, exposing small boulders lined with roots like twisted, clutching hands reaching up from the dark earth. And for a moment the stones there looked like skulls.

'I heard about the ring, Gage. You should have talked to me first, you know. It might have saved the both of us a lot of heartache.'

He knew what he was hearing, and his body understood right away, because his gut clenched up tight as a snake's asshole, and he felt a sharp, cold beat of pain at the base of his jaw, a rhythmic clock of hurt. Unbidden, his hand slipped into the pocket of his jacket and his fingers slowly caressed the hard corners of the little velvet box.

'Oh, Mellie. I thought you'd be happy. And you woulda been, I guess. But something happened, didn't it? Was it that Yankee boy? That Larry?'

Melanie didn't turn, just kept on looking out at the river, at the slow rush of water, with the fat moon swimming in its own reflection and touching the faint currents with cold light. Up to her left the skeletal girders of the river bridge hung across the water like machine-tooled steel bones. The water smelled green and chilly, and breathed mist here and there above its surface. Laughter sounded away down the river, distant and slightly hysterical.

'How do you know about him?' she asked softly.

He stood up and lumbered towards her. 'Don't matter, does it? I heard, that's all. Little bird told me, maybe. Listen, don't you even want to see it?'

'See what?'

'The ring, Mellie. The ring I got for you. Here, look.'

He came up next to her, his hand outstretched, the open box in the centre of his palm. The diamond chip sparkled in the shadows of his palm, a cold blue splinter of light. She looked down at it, then shook her head and looked away.

'I wish you hadn't showed me that, Gage.'

'Why, Mellie? Does it make you feel bad? But why would that be? If you can run off with some hippy Jew boy and not even say one word to me, I guess looking at the ring old fool Gage bought for you shouldn't bother you none. Should it? Mellie?'

'Gage . . . I'm sorry. But it wasn't Larry, really. Things . . . just weren't gonna work out, and I figured it was better to let them go. You know?'

'I don't understand. Why wouldn't things work out? Was it something I did? You could of told me that, couldn't you?'

She felt a sudden urge to just throw herself into the water, sink deep and let the current take her, carry her off to some place where things weren't so hard. Poor old Gage. But she didn't love him, did she?

'Gage, I said I'm sorry. It wasn't you, really. But it wouldn't work. Blame me all you want. It's my fault, I guess. I'm just not ready.'

But he seized on that with the strength of a drowning man. 'Oh, is that it? Well, I guess I can understand. You're only sixteen. Maybe that is too young – though a lot of you Hankings girls tied the knot by then. Your mama for one. But maybe things has changed some, and if you want to wait a while, I'm willing.'

She felt his need, felt his bottomless capacity for self-deception, and finally understood there was no easy way of getting this thing done.

'Put it away,' she whispered.

'Huh?'

'Put that ring away, Gage. It's no use, I ain't going to marry you, not now, not in two years, or ten, for that matter. You understand me? I didn't want to be this plain about it, but you don't want to listen. It's over, Gage. I don't want to see you any more. You can take the ring back to the jewelry store. They'll give you your money back.'

He stood for the space of five long heartbeats, frozen, his hand stretched out like some cast-iron yard dummy, and then he made a funny little clicking noise deep in his throat. She saw the flash of movement out of the corner of her eye, and automatically tracked the arc of the square box, still open, its tiny diamond cargo glinting with each slow roll, until it fell with an almost silent splash out towards the middle of the river.

'Gage! You lost your mind?'

'Lost something,' Gage snarled thickly. 'Lost you, I guess. Lost my own self-respect, too. So I guess you owe me something, Mellie Hankings. And I aim to collect it before I leave this place tonight.'

A slow, sludgy fear began to congeal in her belly, in the thick muscles of her thighs. 'What you talking about?'

She felt his hands close on her upper arms from behind, one on each side. She'd never realized just how big he was. It was like being caught in a huge, padded vice.

'You know what I'm talking about . . .'

Lucas could make the GTO go quiet as honey dripping from a hive when he felt like it, almost no sound at all, just the silent vibrations of power shaking the car like an invisible bass guitar. He was doing it now, as he pulled up just before the river bridge and punched off his lights.

Gravel crunched beneath the fat tires. He switched off the ignition and listened to the night. After a few moments, the sounds grew clearer and he was able to sort them out from the formless background of croaking frogs, whispering water, and wind rattling through the soft leaves.

He leaned back in the bucket seat, clasped his hands behind his head, and turned his face up to the moon. That pale, sharp bone-light caught every crease and ledge of his face and, for a moment, he looked like one of those ancient stone idols, something dug up from bitter earth, from a grave full of broken bones. Something eternally hungry, buried within the circle of its own sacrifices.

He waited until he judged the time was right, then got out of the car. His boots made no sound as he walked across the gravel, so smoothly he seemed to float, like the mist drifting across the black water below.

He was smiling.

If she'd ever thought about such a thing, it would have been in the mythic southern terms of what a good woman *should* feel. A good woman, if some sex pervert *was* raping her, would feel nothing, because a good woman could only be violated against her will, and her body would rebel against that, would turn off its senses and its nerves and deny the beast anything but the unresponsive meat. Ideally, the good woman would faint.

Of course it was all lies. She felt everything.

She felt small sharp stones grind into her back. She felt his weight on her like a mattress. She smelled the sharp, vinegary stink of him, the foul, broken-toothed stench of his mouth, the acrid taste of the Red Man chew tobacco he favoured, and the vomitously explosive remnants of the whiskey he'd taken to fortify himself for this night.

His stubbled cheeks scraped like sandpaper against her, an agony. Bracelets of dark fire constricted her wrists where he squeezed her. She could feel the small bones in there grinding against each other.

The dank breeze off the river turned her naked skin to goosebumps, made the red ligatures where he'd torn her blouse off her body feel etched with fire. He had ripped the zipper out of her jeans as he'd yanked them down. They bound her legs as effectively as ropes, so she couldn't even kick at him.

He grunted like a hog, his breath raspy with lust as he heaved himself upon her.

She gasped, tried to scream, that pain was like nothing she'd ever felt. 'No . . .' she moaned, but his fist was rammed in her mouth, smashing her lips against her teeth, and she tasted her own blood mixed in with his rank musk.

His jagged, brutal rhythm grew faster, more frenzied. His foul, hot breath seared her eyes, her nostrils, filled her mouth, as his beard flayed the skin on her cheeks and chin into rawness.

He was coming on to his moment now, she knew, she tried to beat her fists against his back, but she might as well have been pounding the side of an elephant for all the good it did. And somehow this was the worst, that he would leave his unwanted seed inside her as if she were nothing more than a scumbag, that she had lost the purity she'd once had, and for this. To this . . .

'No . . . no . . .'

A slow shudder began to rise in him, and she closed her eyes.

'Hello, Gage. Nice night for spooning, huh? You romantic old devil, you.'

*   *   *

Mellie felt him freeze on her, his great weight still crushing her, but he had raised his greasy head and was staring at something she couldn't see. From her vantage point, all she could make out was the bottom of his whiskery chin, the shelf of his yellow teeth, and the two hairy pits of his nostrils.

She heard a voice that sounded horribly close to laughter say, 'Gage, old buddy, you sure do have a hand with the ladies, don't you? I'd have never thought it, if I hadn't seen it with my own two eyes.'

'Lucas, get the fuck away from here.' Gage's own voice was rough with heat and fatigue and the remnants of lust. It reminded her of the sound an old whipped dog would make, if you pulled it off its prey. A fierce joy ran through her then.

'Kill him, Lucas!' she spat out. '*Kill* the raping sonofabitch bastard!'

But he only chuckled softly. 'Sorry, darlin'. I don't think that was part of our deal. You could let me check the fine print, though, and I'll get right back to you.'

She felt Gage's immense bulk roll off her. It was as if the earth itself had been lifted away, and for a moment she just lay there, her chest heaving as she tried to suck all the night air into her breath-starved lungs.

After a minute she hitched herself over onto her side. She moaned softly, then bit her lip to keep from gasping. She resolved to die right there in front of Gage Temple, rather than let him see how bad he'd hurt her.

'Here, darlin', let me help you up.' She felt Lucas's hand gently brush her shoulder, but he was a man, and right then she was resolved that no man would ever lay so much as a finger on her again.

'*Get* your filthy hands off me!'

He drew back. 'Oops, Mellie, sorry about that. Mite touchy tonight, aren't we?'

'You sonofabitch,' she said dully, pushing herself to her hands and knees, then pausing, her sweat-soaked hair hanging down the sides of her face in thick, clotted strings. For some reason she couldn't seem to get any further than that.

The damnedest things started running through her mind as she held there, panting like a dog. For some reason she thought about some of the pamphlets and articles she'd read in the lady's magazines – about how you weren't even supposed to *call* them lady's magazines any more – and about these strange new women's movements beginning to flourish, mostly in the cities, of course, and mostly up north. She'd read an article by a woman whose picture next to the title made her look like a dried-out old prune, but what she wrote had made a lot of sense, or seemed to. It was about rape, and how everybody thought rape had to do with sex, it was just sex maniacs, but this woman said no, it was about violence. It was no different than a man going up to a woman and beating her with a club. The principle was the same. To hurt, to punish.

The idea of that had made sense to Mellie when she'd read it, but she didn't really feel the arterial truth of it until this very moment, on her hands and knees before a man who had just used his cock like a club on her, to bruise and tear and punish. And so she learned something she hadn't known before, about men and the beasts that could live beneath their skins, and a dark reason why some of them did what they did.

'Gage Temple,' she said, low and fervent through the blood that coated her bruised lips. 'I ain't your whipping girl, and I never will be.'

But he wasn't listening. She heard him say something, but it wasn't to her, or about her, though at first she thought it was.

'You!' was what he said.

Very close to midnight of that same night, the Reverend Buck gave up wrestling on his own with the problem of his son. He had not been satisfied with the outcome of the previous Thursday dinner. In fact, if anything, he was more worried. All day Friday he had scurried around, called in more than a few favours, made phone calls, even driven out and talked to old Evan Hunter, who had once been the biggest real estate wheeler dealer in these parts, and what he discovered was, to put it mildly, disconcerting.

His son, with no help from him whatsoever was, at the age of twenty, worth at least two and a half million dollars. When he thought about that sum, his forehead grew prickly and damp, and he said 'Whew!' and fanned himself with his hand.

Those quarters had added up indeed.

They had added up to some fairly large parcels of property out along the south edge of town, purchased under the name Renaissance Properties, which had turned out to be a shell company owned by another shell company that was, basically, Lucas's bank accounts.

He had half a million or so in cash, spread around the local banks, most of the accounts less than twenty thousand dollars. Good thinking, Preacher Buck applauded. Fully insured by the Federal Deposit Insurance Corporation, God bless the United States government.

Not that he was sure it mattered. It looked as if Lucas just might *own* the Merchant's National, where the Preacher had a small and obscure percentage, and something called Renaissance Investments, Ltd, had a much larger, though equally shy and retiring, piece. Fifty-four percent, actually.

And he was still waiting to hear from what

contacts and sources he had in Wilmington, Baltimore and, incredibly, New York City.

It was conceivable that Lucas was richer than he was.

And that was indeed a problem, for in what the Reverend Buck rather cynically viewed as the inevitable battle for Lucas's soul (How could you battle for something that had never existed?), he, being one of the battlers, had expected to have the advantage of that great leveller and lever – cold, hard cash – on his side. But this was evidently not to be.

He was out on the back porch, his solid bulk wrapped in an old white terrycloth bathrobe so well used its nap had worn almost smooth from Marie's washing, and, though clean as a tick, it had become a soft ivory colour. He wore a pair of leather bedroom slippers, flannel lined, that had moulded themselves over the years to the shape of his feet and the way his toenails humped up thick and yellow at the ends, like damned turtle shells or something.

He tossed off the dregs of the Blanton's at the bottom of his glass, then set it down on the table next to his rocker. It was the last night of the full moon, and he could see her out there, riding low above the orchard, playing shadow games. Well, he'd been putting it off long enough, but he supposed he'd better get to it.

'And if that isn't the truth . . .' he remarked to the

night air as he tilted the rocker forward until his feet were flat on the worn planks of the porch floor. He let his momentum carry him on upright; then he flip-flopped over to the back porch railing and paused, for an instant unwilling to go further, even though he knew it was necessary.

The smell of the tulip beds planted below wafted up and filled his nose, and he smiled faintly. Finally, with a soft groan of effort, he climbed down the three steep wooden back steps and began to make his way through the apple and cherry and peach trees, towards the corroded old iron-pipe gate set into the bobwire fence at the back.

'It wasn't no damned hippy, it was you, wasn't it Lucas? I knew she wouldn't toss me over for no Jew boy Yankee. But for you, mister high and mighty Lucas Buck? Of course she would. Did you get yourself a good deal? I bet you did. The bitch.'

He spoke so fast and furiously that threads of spit flew from his lips and gleamed on his chin and cheeks. He finished hitching his pants up, zipping them, and pulling the heavy belt through its big silver-brass buckle with the golden 'g' on it. Lucas stood about six feet away, watching him. Gage made a snuffling sound. Both men ignored the girl on her hands and knees.

'Hey, Gage, what can I tell you? The Beatles lied. Money *can* buy you love.'

'You son of a bitch. Well, if you want her, you can have her. I already wiped my dick on her, she's used trash. You keep that in mind, Lucas. And as far as it goes, I think I'll give you a little something else to keep in mind.'

'Oh? What would that be, Gage?'

Gage's big hands dropped again to his belt. He unbuckled it and slowly drew the snaky, salt-whitened leather from the loops around his waist. He let the heavy buckle fall, then swung the leather back and forth, experimentally, in a pair of whip-like strokes. Everybody knew that Gage kept the edges of that buckle honed to a razor's edge.

'Put my mark on you, Lucas. Just like I did her.'

'Now, Gage, you don't want to get all carried away over this.'

But Gage only shook his head, whipped the belt in a vicious circle one more time, and said, 'Fuck you, Lucas. Here I come.'

He lunged forward and fell flat on his face. Mellie saw the last part. Her mouth slowly dropped open. She had heard a sound like a mush-melon falling off the table onto the floor, a sharp, wet, squishy sound. Gage let out a whooshing sigh, quivered once, and lay still.

Lucas chuckled. 'Dumb as a post, that boy. You see that, Mellie? Took off his damn belt and look there. He never did get his pants fastened right, and wouldn't you know they'd fall down to his knees and trip him right up? Looks like he cracked his thick skull a good one, too.'

Lucas shook his head, ambled over to Gage's prone form, squatted, and put his fingers on Gage's bullish neck. 'Ticker's pumping away OK, feels like. Guess he'll live.'

He stood up, slapped his hands together and made washing motions. 'You ready to go yet, Mellie? I'd be happy to give you a ride.' He glanced around. 'Seems to me this party's just about over, anyway.'

The rusty metal of the rotten old gate felt wet and cold to his hand – but then, it always did. Preacher Buck had to give it a pretty good push; the bottom of the gate was stuck in the dirt. It didn't seem to matter how often he came down here, the gate was always cold, damp, and stuck.

And it always finally swung open with a sudden sharp shriek, as if his strength was an agony to the corroded metal. He shut the gate behind him, shaking his head. Funny damned things he was starting to think about these days, especially down here in the old cemetery. Perhaps not such a good sign, all things considered.

What path there had been through his orchard vanished entirely on the other side of the gate. Here the chokecherry bushes and rambler roses that were mostly stickers abounded, along with pods of milkweed, nodding stalks of Queen Anne's lace, plantain, stands of poison ivy, and a surf of dark green kudzu climbing the twisted trunks of a few dying oak trees.

The gravestones were hidden everywhere. If you weren't careful, you would bark your shins on the tipsy, moss-grey old slabs. He made his way through as much by memory and feel as anything else, until he stood in the centre of the ancient graveyard.

Here was a kind of clearing where wild grass grew ankle deep around a couple of gravestones so old they were worn entirely smooth – though coated like all the others with a skin of dry, flaking mould – and a single weathered boulder half buried in the ground. The grass felt dry and repellent on the naked, blue-veined flesh of his ankles, like being gently stroked by hordes of insect feelers.

There was something about the shape of the larger stone that unsettled the eye, especially in the clinical light of the moon. A peculiar, almost organic lumpiness, as if either the stone was trying to pop from the ground like the core of a nasty pimple, or something inside the stone itself was trying to do the same thing.

Preacher Buck looked up at the sky. The moon was still there, a bloated, obscenely yellow orb, like a balloon full of pus, but now ragged shreds of cloud, like fat spiderwebs, began to flood across the sky. Preacher Buck couldn't be certain, but he doubted that the sky was pulling such tricks anywhere outside the graveyard. Over the years he'd come around to the idea that this cemetery, wherever it might seem to be, wasn't exactly where the rest of the world was. The weather here, for instance, seemed to have a mind of its own.

As he settled himself on the boulder, a ghost wind began to rise, low and moaning, rattling the gnarled branches of the oaks and shaking the dry milkweeds like a dice cup full of bones. In the space of a moment or two the temperature dropped perhaps twenty degrees. The Reverend put the palms of his big hands on his knees and wished he'd thought to wear something a little warmer than a bathrobe and bedroom slippers.

This was the hardest part, the waiting. He sat, very conscious of the ebb and flow of blood through his veins, feeling the chill creep into the tips of his fingers and toes, and the wind whining through all the trashwood undergrowth.

After a while it began to happen: at first a faint intimation, the slightest hot kiss of breath across his cheeks. He nodded to himself and said, 'Yeah, I'm here.'

There was no obvious reply, but now the levels of the air seemed to settle out into two distinct layers; dank and cold from his chest on down, but rank, hot, and humid above that. For a moment he wondered if his *body* was somehow split into two different places, but he pushed that thought away as quickly as he could. He didn't want to think about such things, because if he did, then he might start thinking about—

No.

He squeezed his knees hard, swallowed, and waited. And after a while they began to come, just as he'd known they would. The sickly yellow light of the moon vanished behind a suffocating screen of bruised-looking clouds, and the vines and creepers and stunted trees took on a slick, phosphorescent sheen, like the tumescent, swollen belly of a week-dead river carp. The stone on which he sat felt suddenly hot, and the two obscenely smooth gravestones, like misshapen phalluses thrusting erect from the earth, began to glow with some hellish, flesh-coloured inner light.

He closed his eyes, the better to see things that no longer existed in the world, but only in the eye of his inner mind. Shifting, twisting shapes, drifting aimlessly, caught forever between what they had left, and the place they feared to go. He knew them, and why should he not? He'd served them all his life, and his father before him, and on back as far as the seed of the Buck men went in this place. And someday, when his own time was done, his son Lucas would serve them too.

Christopher Buck was not much of an introspective man, and he hadn't thought about this for many years. He almost never thought about how it had come to be, though at one time he'd known it with the same bone-deep certainty he'd known his own name. For it didn't matter, did it? Whatever deals had been made, eight or nine or ten generations ago, those deals were ancient history, and had served both sides well. Why think about them now? It was two hundred years too late for that.

'Ahhh . . .' he whispered, as their great wings, stealthy as death by drowning, enfolded him. They were in him now, and he in them, like the voodoo riders from the hot islands and the hidden swamps.

A certain amount of time passed, and when that was done with, and he had figured out what he would have to do about Lucas, Preacher Buck raised his arms to the swollen, crepuscular clouds overhead. Then it turned to horror, pure and simple.

Lucas stood in the dark and watched Melanie drag herself to her feet, knowing better now than to try to help her in any way. It was quite a performance on her part, and he admired her for it. The strength and resilience of the human spirit, though always doomed to fail in the end, fascinated him. And now *she* fascinated him as she finally inched all the way up, then bent over and hitched up her torn jeans and held them around her waist with one hand. With the other she tried as best she could to pin the tattered rags of her blouse closed.

'Mellie, there's a sweater up in the car, in the back seat. You feel free, OK?'

She glanced at him, nodded, then turned quickly away. He watched her go, sighed, then looked down at Gage. When he was sure she was well beyond earshot, his lips drew back and he murmured, 'Thought we had a deal, Gage, you dirty old boy, you.'

Then he kicked the prone form as hard as he could, just once. He heard ribs breaking in there, a dry and muffled snap like twigs cracking inside a soft leather bag. He smiled even wider. 'Maybe next time you'll remember a deal's a deal, my impetuous redneck friend.'

But Gage only uttered a soft, moist moan, quickly choked off, and after a second or two, Lucas turned away. He ambled over to the edge of the water, stepped out gingerly onto the slick, rounded stones, and squatted.

He reached out and it was there, bobbing in the water, right at the tips of his fingers. As he'd known it would be. He fished it out, flipped open the little box, and grinned at the tiny stone winking up at him in its nest of soggy velvet.

'Cheap old thing,' he said to no-one in particular. But he slipped the box into his jacket pocket.

He stepped over Gage Temple's prone body and paused.

'Hell, Gage, I guess I'll put my mark on *you*,' he said, and added another souvenir to his little cache. He didn't see Mellie, who had paused, watch him with wide eyes from the shadows up ahead. Or maybe he did.

Whistling softly, he headed back up the road.

Chapter Seven

Larry Rosenweig cursed himself for being five different kinds of fool, but he couldn't help it. It had been eating at him for the last hundred or so miles, sometimes so bad he would just stop next to whatever road he was walking on, turn away from the traffic, and shout, 'No! Stop *thinking* about it!'

But he couldn't. For some perverse reason, the further away he got from Trinity, South Carolina, the more what had happened there ballooned up inside his thoughts until it crowded almost everything out and he would find himself facing backwards to cars whizzing by, the hot, gassy breath of their slipstream twitching at the collar of his jean jacket as he muttered and shouted at himself.

He knew people must have thought he was crazy. Hell, *he* thought he was crazy. But what he thought didn't make a dime's worth of difference, because slowly he was coming to understand that his life was hanging in the balance. As he was beginning to see the equation, he could do the right thing, the sane and rational thing, and turn his face to the north, stick out his thumb, and keep on going until he hit New York City and looked up his old buddy Woozer Collins, who'd already said he would put him up till he could find a job and a place of his own.

That was the sane thing. And if he did it, he was fairly certain he would not be able to look at himself in his shaving mirror without remembering what it felt like to have his own hot piss running down his leg, standing in the middle of a strip of blacktop two miles outside of Trinity. And not for the next week or month or so. For the rest of his entire fucking life.

Lucas Buck.

No, if he was going to do that, better he should turn west right now, see if he could hook a big Peterbilt heading for back home again in In-deee-ana, where it seems that I can see. See my future plain enough, he thought, a job in the paper mill, kiss all those flabby white gentile cheeks and maybe, just maybe, my pop's money will someday be good enough for me to buy myself a house in Brentwood Estates.

And I would rather buy a *grave* there, he thought, since if I do go back, that is exactly what I'll be doing. So, now what?

There was always the third option, the crazy one. But the more he turned it over in his mind, the more he gave it yet another mental polish, the more it seemed to take on an irresistible glow. In the end, he was coming to the idea that if he let that light grow large enough, it might crowd out that other, awful thing that seemed to be filling up his skull.

The incontrovertible truth of the matter, he realized, was that he'd lost something, left it lying in the dust along that misbegotten stretch of road beyond the Trinity River Bridge. And the only way he was going to get it back was to turn around, catch one of those cars with the licence plates that proclaimed 'Florida – the *Sunshine* State!' until he got to the place where he had lost it, and find it again.

Not so long before, the Jews in Israel had taken on just about every Arab country that could field some kind of army, and not only had they survived, but they'd damn near conquered the entire Middle East. He'd been just past his bar mitzvah (*now you are a man . . .*), and he had thrilled to the accounts of what his brothers – and he thought of them that way, his brave brothers and sisters – what they had done over there. As if somehow it made up for the shamefulness of all the millions who had shuffled docilely off to the ovens twenty-five years before. He knew he wasn't supposed to think of what the Nazis had done as shameful for the Jews, but he did. Blissful in his simple ignorance of a complicated history, he knew he would have killed himself a bunch of Nazis before he went, that was for sure.

So now, what were his choices? Easy enough. He could keep on for New York and see if he really could stand looking in the mirror after a while, or he could put his head down and shuffle docilely off to the good old Hoosier state.

Or he could live up to a freshly minted heritage from that forge of modern Jewish history, the great Middle Eastern Arab Asskicking, and see if that fucking peckerwood Lucas Buck and his cornhole-licking weasel of a sidekick, Ben Healy, would like to have another go-round with Larry Whatsisname, a real *fighting* Jew.

Rosenweig, he told himself. He could almost hear the trumpets pealing victoriously offstage. They call me *Mister* Rosenweig!

Anyway, this wasn't the Nazis he was talking about, or even the Arabs. Just some southern rednecks. After all, he thought, unaware that he was grinding his teeth so hard his jaw would ache for a week: what are they gonna do, kill me?

As usual, the good ladies of the First Trinity Baptist Auxiliary heard about Preacher Buck's idea before anybody else. It was called the Lady's Auxiliary, not the Women's, because no self-respecting decent southern female thought of herself as a *woman*, at least not as first definition, and certainly not publicly (most of them thought of a woman as only a lady reduced to her basic biological function, as in: a woman of the streets). A woman was what she was. A lady was how she behaved.

Marie Fairthingale, the Preacher's housekeeper, was not above letting drop a few choice nuggets gleaned from her daily duties, as long as, in her judgement, no harm was done. And since the Preacher had asked her opinion, and hadn't seemed secretive about it at all, she guessed he wouldn't mind if she spread it around a bit. He had, in fact, asked her what she thought the other ladies would think, if they would support the idea. Well, there was only one way to find out about that . . .

'Why, Marie, I think that is just a *wonderful* idea. You say Preacher Buck wants to do it?' said Thelma Ritter in that breathy, little-girl way of speaking she had.

There were four ladies from the auxiliary gathered around their usual table-booth in the rear of the Elks Lodge restaurant, which was open to the public, and which served the best chocolate malts and pounded pork tenderloin sandwiches in the town of Trinity. It was to this table these four ladies repaired, regular as clockwork, at four o'clock every Wednesday after the meeting of the Auxiliary Steering Committee.

In theory, the Steering Committee meeting, which consisted of anywhere from eight to eleven elected women, had the final say on what was what with the Auxiliary itself. The meetings of the committee were open to anyone who cared to attend, and much business was transacted by a simple show of hands.

Which was all well and good, except that, like many things in Trinity, all was not as it appeared with the Baptist Lady's Auxiliary. The truth of the matter was that the real Wednesday meeting took place *after* the public meeting, and this meeting was private, secluded, and conducted over ritual malts, sundaes, and banana splits in the back of the Elks Lodge restaurant. Marie Fairthingale had been presiding over these meetings, by virtue of her close association with Preacher Buck, for going on twenty years now.

Thelma Ritter, who had just finished up her formal vow of support – unnecessary, everybody understood, because if Preacher Buck wanted the Lady's Auxiliary's support for something, that support would be forthcoming. And no questions would be asked.

'Yes, Thelma, that's what he said. He was sitting in his little office – I'd just finished tidying the papers on his desk – next Sunday's sermon – and running some Pledge across the top.' (Marie liked to throw out these little insider details by way of adding lustre to the provenance of whatever she was about to say.) 'He looked up from the book he was reading, and flat out asked me about it. I was a little surprised, I have to admit. Usually he, you know, tries to feel me out about his ideas, first.'

All four ladies quirked their lips in small chuckles at the – conceivably off-colour – reference to the Reverend Buck *feeling out* Marie Fairthingale, even though they all knew Marie was a good ten years past any such foolishness. Well, all of them knew that except for Marie. What Marie knew was that the mutual feeling out process which had begun five years before, a few months after Preacher Buck lost his dear wife Hester in that tragic accident, was still going on, hot as ever. And wouldn't this crew of snickering old biddies just about wet their undies if they knew about that?

'Thelma, I think he is very serious about this. Very serious,' Marie said. 'And I think we should put our heads together, right now, and see what we can do to help.'

Leola Granger, called Lolly, clicked open her black patent leather purse and took out a small spiral ring notebook with a green cardboard cover, and a transparent Bic pen with a blue cap. 'I'll take notes, so we don't forget,' she announced in her brisk, no-nonsense voice. In her mid-forties, she was the youngest of the four, though she'd led a hard life before her husband, Cecil, shuffled off this mortal coil. Thank God good old Cece, evil bastard though he undeniably had been, had believed in life insurance. Lolly knew she had Preacher Buck's work to thank for that, him urging

Cecil to spend some of the loot on a set of good insurance policies.

It turned out that he'd bought two hundred thousand worth of whole life four months before the cerebral accident led to his passing. Lolly tried to regard it as an unfortunate passing, but could never even think those words together without having to repress a sudden fit of giggles.

Cecil had gone the way of many men after a vascular blowout, planting his Coupe de Ville into a palmetto swamp at seventy-five miles an hour while on a business trip to Atlanta. Double indemnity, of course, though the insurance company had first tried to squabble about it being the stroke that killed him, not the wreck, but Preacher Buck had even taken care of that.

Because of all this, the widow Granger had few worries, none of them financial. She tended to devote a great deal of time and energy to the doings of the Auxiliary, and a great deal of loyalty to anything that Preacher Buck might desire.

Thelma Ritter, older, but also flightier, fluttered fingers bearing many rings in Lolly Granger's direction. 'Yes, Lolly, that's a good idea, why don't you write everything down? I just have so much trouble remembering everything these days.' She pronounced it day-*yuz*, and batted her eyelashes again.

Lolly gave her a flinty, sideways glance that spoke, far better than words, just what Lolly thought of Thelma, who'd most likely been out shopping when God was passing out the grey matter that should have been beneath her I-Love-Lucy coloured hair.

Georgina Hendricks, the quietest, though in some ways the most influential of the four, spoke up at last. She'd just turned fifty, though she looked younger, but something about that milestone had made her start to think about life a little deeper than she ever had before, and the other women had noted a change in her personality because of it. Georgina sometimes seemed to think almost like a man.

'Take a heap of money,' she said, 'to build another war memorial in the square. And for only three of our boys, all told. Might be better just to add another plaque to the Great War one.'

Marie eyed her. If you wanted to talk about money, Georgina was the one who had it. Her brother was Evan Hunter, who had made two or three fortunes in local real estate, much of it in partnership with Howie Hendricks, his brother-in-law. With old Howie now safely in the ground for six years, what with income, interest and all, Marie guessed that Georgina was at least a millionaire. Or would that be millionairess?

Either way, if Georgina was to get solidly behind the idea, a lot of things that might not get done otherwise would get done.

'Georgina, dear, we know that,' Marie said

smoothly. 'But it's such a worthy cause. And it's only three boys *now*, so of course we could think about adding to the War Memorial. But the Reverend says he is *certain* there'll be more, and it's better to be prepared in advance than to scrabble around at the last minute when the body bags start to pile up.'

At that, perhaps shocked at what her inner ear had just heard herself say, Marie blushed right through her three layers of Max Factor and decided to let somebody else carry the ball for a while.

But the other ladies understood the blunt way of speaking that came over Marie every now and again, and were used to it. No, it wasn't ladylike, exactly, but on occasion it did serve to cut through the bullshit, though none of them, not even Marie herself, would have said that out loud.

'Well,' Georgina said at last. 'You may have a point. But surely that nice Mister Nixon isn't going to let that terrible war go on forever? After all, he's promised.'

Marie raised one iron-grey eyebrow, as if to give her opinion of politicians and anything they might promise. Georgina caught it all right, and nodded. 'As I say, you may have a point, Marie. It's worth looking into, I do agree to that.'

Lolly stuck the tip of her tongue out of the corner of her mouth and made a small checkmark next to Georgina Hendricks's name in her book. To outside ears, Georgina might not sound all that enthusiastic, but as far as the ladies gathered at the table heard, she'd just delivered a ringing endorsement of Preacher Buck's plan for the Trinity Vietnam Veteran's Memorial Project.

Marie turned to Thelma now. There were those who knew of the existence – and purpose – of this group that always met on Wednesdays after the Auxiliary meeting, and whether they approved or not, most wondered how Thelma Ritter fitted into it. After all, it seemed she brought very little to the table. Marie Fairthingale's bona fides were obvious, and few could argue with the sheer power of Georgina Hendricks's money – she was, after all, the richest independent female in Fulton County. Even Lolly Granger was an easy fit – aside from money of her own, most ladies in Trinity did respect her formidable intelligence. But Thelma Ritter? Now that was a hard one to understand. She had little money, less intelligence, a husband, Harold, whose significance in the general scheme of things was even lower than her own, and, finally, a personality generally agreed to rub most people the wrong way.

Marie knew all this, but like all good generals, she knew a bit more. Thelma Ritter, locked out of the group, could have caused it great damage. For she did possess one overwhelming talent, though most folks wouldn't have called it exactly that. But she was as good a gossip as Marie had ever seen or heard of. Had the other three women stonewalled Thelma about the doings of their little group, she would have made it her business to leak, second-guess, chatter about, denigrate, and otherwise keep a witch's pot of rumour, scandal, and hearsay permanently abubble.

On the inside, however, as one of the ladies of Wednesday afternoon, her rather amazing talents could be properly harnessed for the good of the cause, rather than the ill. And so, with a secret understanding that she was now cocking and aiming an already loaded gun, Marie said, 'Thelma, dear?'

'Yes, Marie?'

'I think it would be a good idea if you sort of . . . checked around. You know, made a few telephone calls, perhaps made a point of mentioning the idea when you do your shopping? You know what I mean, just to check out the lay of the land. I know it's a trial for you to just go out and talk to people, but perhaps just this once . . .'

'Oh, of course. That's just a marvellous idea, Marie.' She paused, a sudden expression of false modesty weighing down her overloaded black eyelashes. 'If you're sure you trust me to do things up right, I mean?'

Marie smiled at her, while stonily thinking that she would trust Thelma Ritter with the job of derailing the invasion of Normandy Beach, if it came right down to it. 'Thelma, of course I trust you. Have you ever let us down yet?'

Lolly Granger made another checkmark in her little book, and wondered if anybody really understood the assault the Trinity telephone system was about to undergo. Well, think of it whatever way one would, by the time the four of them gathered in this spot a week hence, they would have an excellent idea of who favoured, and more important, who didn't favour, the Reverend Buck's idea to build a Vietnam Memorial in the Trinity town square.

Marie signalled the end of this *ad hoc* meeting of the real rulers of the Baptist Lady's Auxiliary by hoisting her own large brown leather handbag from the floor, opening it, and taking out her change purse. She pursed her lips and clicked it open.

'Thelma,' she said, 'you had the banana split. That's fifty- five cents, I believe . . .'

Lucas had dropped Melanie off at the curb in front of her parents' house. He had not spoken to her, except to nod at the fact that she had pulled his big, shapeless sweater over the top of her ruined blouse. Then he said, 'You think your mama and daddy will give you any trouble?'

She had looked at him for several long seconds, not really knowing why, but discovering that if she expected him to drop his own gaze before the ferocious pain of her own, she was mistaken. He only stared back at her, the moist surface of his eyes catching the occasional glint of the moon, which turned them weird and silvery, until she lowered her eyes and stared at her hands, fingers twisting like a nest of blind albino snakes in her lap.

'That you, Mellie?' her mother called softly from the front parlour, as Melanie scurried past and headed on up the stairs for the safety of her bedroom.

She paused, half way up the steps, one hand on the worn pine bannister, the other still holding the snap of her ruined jeans together. 'It's me, Mama.'

In the background, she could hear the raucous, snort-ghock-gasp-wheeze of Joshua Hankings, sawing off a big one, as Heppy liked to put it. Heppy said, 'That Gage Temple drop you off?'

Melanie knew Heppy's eyes had not missed one trick, and that the older woman knew exactly whose car had stopped to let her off in front of the house.

'No, Mama. It was Lucas Buck.'

'What happened to Gage?'

'His old Plymouth broke down, and he called Lucas to give me a ride.'

'Huh,' Heppy said non-committally. 'Gage said he wanted to talk to you. You get all your talkin' done?'

'Yes, Mama.'

'Well . . . ?'

'I'm real tired, Mama. I'll tell you in the morning.'

She waited then, but evidently Heppy was satisfied, for all she could hear was what sounded like the strangulation of pigs, as her daddy started sawing off another good one.

She didn't actually break down and cry until she'd made it all the way to the top of the stairs, down the hall, and safely behind the door of the room she'd once shared with Christine what now seemed like a million years ago.

When she was young.

When Gage Temple woke up the next day, his first thought was that he'd been in a car wreck or some such awful thing. It was just before dawn, the sky a flat, slug-like grey beyond the smeared glass of his window, and he had that odd, gluey feeling of just awakening and not being exactly sure where he was, or how he'd gotten there. But wherever he was, he wasn't alone. Somebody was watching . . .

He sat bolt upright, flinging sweat-soaked sheets away from himself like Lazarus thrashing out of his graveclothes. He choked back an involuntary screech as something like a dagger twisted sharply in his side.

'Who's there?' he whispered. 'Who is that?'

He heard something rustle in the shadows

beyond the bed, where the murk piled up in the corners. Frantically he groped for something he could use as a weapon; his eyes bulged.

'I said, *who is that!*'

'Huh? Uh . . .'

He knew that voice, and suddenly he felt like an idiot. 'Marvis? Is that you, you rootsucking sonofabitch?'

'Aw . . . morning, Gage. Nice way to talk.' Slowly, Marvis's emaciated form congealed in the gloom as he got up from the chair he'd been dozing in, and stepped toward the bed, into the uncertain light from the window.

'I see you,' Gage said, relief suddenly flooding him. He flopped back down, put one hand on his forehead, winced, and let out a moan.

'What the hell happened to me, Marvis?'

'I dunno, Gage. I got a call from Lucas Buck to drive out to the fuck place down by the river, and so I did, and there you were.'

Gage closed his eyes. Behind them, something awful was beginning to move out of the merciful fog that had hidden it. 'Lucas Buck called you?'

'Uh huh. He weren't exactly chatty, but he said you'd be out there, and probably not real happy, and he was right on both counts.'

Gage could remember very little of the night before. 'Marvis, I feel like I got a busted rib or two, and my head hurts to beat the band, but to tell you

God's truth, mostly I feel half way between drunk and hungover. Now how is that?'

'Oh.' Marvis shuffled up to the bed, poked around, and lifted up an empty glass canning jar from the yellowed, stinking sheets. 'You and me, Gage, we finished her. It was setting right next to where I found you, out to the river. I figgered Lucas musta left it, for some reason or other. Nice of him, wasn't it?'

Marvis grinned, exposing cracked and blackened teeth and a couple of stumps. Gage sighed, started to shake his head, thought better of it and caught himself, then sighed again.

'No wonder m'mouth feels like Dad's old drawers.'

'Gage?'

'What?'

'What'n the hell happened out there?'

Gage stared up at him. 'Lucas Buck made himself an enemy, that's what.'

Marvis stepped back a couple of paces. 'You don't want to be saying that, Gage. Lucas, he's OK.'

Gage's eyes turned hard at that. 'If Lucas is OK for you, Marvis, then you ain't OK for me. You know? So you got to make a choice, I guess. And you better hurry up, 'cause my patience about anything having to do with Lucas Buck is plain and simple gone. So, which is it gonna be – me? Or him?'

'Oh, hell, Gage, we been friends all our lives. Lucas don't mean nothing to me.'

'Good, then. You with me?'

'With you about what? Lucas?'

'Uh huh.'

'I guess so, Gage. What you got in mind?'

'Killin' Lucas Buck.'

'Oh.'

Melanie drew herself a hot bath and stepped in and began to scrub. She took one of the stiff bristle-brushes her mother used on the floors, and filled it with the caustic soap Heppy used when it came time to do the rugs once a year. She was half afraid the combination of the two might just scrape the hide right off her, but in a way, that wasn't such a bad idea. Because her very skin was an abomination, covered with the oil of his body, impregnated with his many stenches, scratched and torn by his teeth and beard and nails.

She thought about that and kept on scrubbing. She rubbed and dubbed and three-men-in-a-tubbed for almost two hours, and when she was done, she was about the colour of Santa Claus's winter coat. But she wasn't quite done yet. Gage hadn't left any surprise packets for her, at least she didn't think so, but he'd had his thing in her.

She thought about that and shuddered, and something vile and bitter belched up out of her and she ran for the toilet and just barely made it. After that she brushed her teeth a couple of times and used up half a bottle of Listerine, till it felt like the whole top of her tongue had blistered up.

Then she opened the special drawer at the side of the sink, the one she shared with her mama (her daddy had looked in there once, said, 'Aw, shit,' closed the drawer and never looked again), and took out the small rubber bag. He'd been in her, all right, and she was going to clean him out, no matter if it took all night.

When at last she could smell nothing on herself but soap, and feel nothing but the heat she'd scrubbed right into her skin, she stopped and let out a long sound of relief. There was one good towel, a souvenir from the Atlanta Mid-South Fair, that was supposed to be a beach towel or something, but Mellie had appropriated it for her own. It was so big and soft and rich feeling.

She worked it with a will, back and forth, a mindless little rhythm to match the chanting voice in the bottom of her mind: 'Gage, gonna kill him. Uh, huh. Gage, gonna kill him. Uh huh!'

Then she went to bed and slept, if not like a baby, at least without any screaming in the night.

Chapter Eight

Thelma Ritter paused in front of the mirror in the downstairs bathroom – what she coyly called the powder room when guests were there and she hid her husband's shaving things below the sink and put out the good towels – and puckered her lips to make sure the Rose Dawn lipstick was holding OK. She turned her head from one side to the other and noted, with approval, that the Ruby Copper cover and frosting she'd had Francine Walters put on down at the Trinity Tease Style Shoppe looked about as natural as she could hope for. Her judgement was a little clouded, because she hadn't seen her real colour for more than ten years. And her makeup was flawless, as it should be. As usual, she'd spent nearly an hour on it. She couldn't exactly explain it, but when she started on one of her little projects, somehow it helped to know she looked as good as she could. Even over the telephone, she believed, people could tell when you were putting your best foot forward.

She tossed herself a wink in the mirror, then flicked off the lights and headed for the kitchen. This was her command centre. She swept in as a general would, with a smart step and an eagle eye for every little detail.

Beyond the far end of the kitchen counter, Harold had taken the plans out of one of his do-it-yourself magazines and built her what he called a message centre. It was a small desk with a drawer beneath and shelves and pigeon holes hanging above, and a telephone and a notepad sitting on the desktop. He'd painted it a pretty avocado colour, and Thelma had bought a comfortable Queen Anne side chair from Engel's Home Furnishings, the nicest furniture store in town, to place in front of it. She thought of it as her command post because, from here, she envisioned herself as the centre of a vast telephonic web that stretched, with exquisite sensitivity, over all of Trinity proper and much of the outlands as well.

Now she poured herself fresh-perked coffee – Folger's Mountain Grown – and placed the delicate little china cup into a matching Lilly Langtry pattern saucer. No mugs with silly sayings on them for her. She made sure she had a freshly sharpened pencil next to her notepad, then leaned back for a second, closed her eyes, and began to plan her campaign.

She decided that thinking about Francine Walters must have been one of those amazing coincidences, because Francine would be the perfect place to start. Francine saw most of the ladies that Thelma wanted to reach, and Francine talked. And though Thelma's mind didn't run to such technical terms, if it had, she would have thought of Francine as an amplifier, the kind that took a little bit of sound and turned it into a continuous roar, like those awful rock and roll bands used. Yes, Francine would be perfect.

She took a sip of coffee – yes, good, Folger's really was the best – and put the tip of her forefinger into the telephone's dial wheel. And as she performed this small act of penetration, a wave of nearly sexual ecstasy suffused her. Almost better than sex, really. Especially sex with Harold.

She dialled. 'Francine? This is Thelma, honey. Have you got a sec to chat . . . ?'

The morning light that flooded into the wide, tall room through windows shielded by gauzy curtains cast a faded, ethereal light on things, like the tint of old photographs. For some reason, no other room in the rambling Victorian castle commanded such light, and Lucas often found himself lingering here early in the day, propped up on a mound of pillows in the huge carved bed, drinking coffee and reading the *Guardian*.

He was doing so now, sections of the paper scattered across the rumpled quilt, listening to the sounds the house made: creaks and faint groans, the protests of wood and stone settling back into the earth from whence they had come, two hundred years before.

He'd been born here, and had lived here all his life. His father had also been born here, and *his* father before him, extending backwards in time to the Buck who had built this place, coincidentally also named Lucas. There was a picture of that Lucas Buck, with his wife, hanging over the fireplace.

But his father had left here five years ago, just after Hester Buck passed on. In this very bedroom, it was said, though the details were still, to this day, hazy, even to Lucas himself.

Whatever had happened, it had driven the Preacher out, and he had taken up residence in the parsonage, which he had previously used only for church entertainment and as a public office. Lucas had opted to stay, and his father had agreed, though some said it was a crime to leave a fifteen-year-old boy on his own like that. Since both Preacher Buck and his son had a conception of crime that would have horrified the livers right out of those naysayers, they found it easy to ignore the gossip.

He was trying, in an absent sort of way, to describe the light in this room. So far, the best he'd been able to come up with was that it was a ghostly light – cool, transparent, evanescent. But ghostly, though it did almost capture the nature of the light, in some inexplicable way fell short, and the true word he sought continued to elude him. Just on the tip of his mind, sort of. He was making yet another half-hearted effort to speak it when the phone on the mahogany stand next to the bed rang sharply.

'Hello?'

'Lucas?'

'Hello, Daddy. What are you up to, this fine morning?'

'Just doing my patriotic bit for Trinity, son. You know.' There was a forced jolliness to the Preacher's tone. Lucas lifted the receiver away from his ear and stared at it for a moment.

'No, I don't know, Daddy. Is it that memorial thing you were talking about?'

'Exactly, Lucas. Some of the ladies have been talking about it, you know. Getting the word out. And I've made a few calls myself. Some people with weight, substantial people. Everybody seems in favour of it.'

Lucas quirked a grin. He knew all about the Preacher's ladies. 'You check with the hippies?'

Preacher Buck snorted. 'Who cares what they think?'

'I might,' Lucas said.

The Preacher fell silent at that, and Lucas listened to the echoing, singing silence of the Trinity phone system. Was it just him, or could he almost hear the sound of Thelma Ritter's voice, whispering away in the background?

'I was afraid you'd say something like that, Lucas. You didn't seem all that enthusiastic when I mentioned it the other day, after we planted Sydney.'

Lucas coughed. 'Well, Daddy, you know, I kind of wonder if Sydney would think it was such a good idea. I bet at the end, he was cussing the day he decided to do his patriotic duty.'

Since they both knew just how and why Sydney had come to join up in the service of his country, the Preacher skated right over that one. Irony was not his strongest suit, though it was a card Lucas could play with surgical precision, and did so far too often for his father's taste.

'Well, boy, here's what I got to say, then. Are you going to support me on this, or not?'

'Can't say yet, Daddy.'

'Maybe we need to have a little talk, then.'

'I thought that's what we were doing right now.'

'No, I mean face to face. And maybe about a few things more than just this memorial thing.'

Lucas raised his coffee mug – on it was a mosquito with the caption 'South Carolina State Bird' – and sipped thoughtfully. 'Like what would that be, Daddy?'

Now the Preacher paused. 'Let's just say a conversation of grave importance, and leave it at that.'

'Grave importance?'

'How about tonight. Come over after dinner, and we'll get this thing thrashed out.'

Lucas watched a gust of wind billow out the white gauze curtains. Ghostly wasn't exactly right, but it was close.

'Sure, Daddy. Eight o'clock.'

'See you then, Lucas.'

Lucas replaced the receiver. He sat for a moment, then finished his coffee with a single gulp, and reached for the phone again.

'I want Wilmington, North Carolina.' He waited, gave a number, then waited some more.

'Good morning, the Renaissance Group. How can we help you?' a firm, pleasant, but utterly feminine voice said.

'Here's what I want you to do . . .' Lucas said.

Ethel Bates was a heavy-set black woman of indeterminate years. If anybody had told her she looked like the pictures of Aunt Jemima she would have whopped them a good one, but secretly, she was rather fond of the comparison. Sure, that old Aunt Jemima was a white thing, with that slave bandanna and all, but people did get a warm feeling when they thought about her. Pancakes and syrup and hot breakfasts, what was so bad about all that?

She fluffed up a pillow on the narrow bed, and said, 'You got a bathroom right down the hall, and I had a real big boiler put in two years back, so there's plenty of hot water. I change the sheets and towels once a week. You want them cleaned more often, you do it yourself. Washer and dryer's in the basement, you leave a dime in the paper cup there for each wash, and a nickel for the dry.'

Ethel paused for breath. She could run through her spiel quick as a raccoon stealing eggs, but it was important that every guest understood the ground rules up front. She might not own the only boarding house on Main Street in Goat Town, but it was the best. Some even said it compared to Loris Holt's place downtown, but Ethel thought that might be stretching things a little.

'Got that so far?' she asked.

The new guest nodded.

'Good. Breakfast is included with the room – family style at the big table in the kitchen downstairs – and supper is fifty cents extra, you let me know that morning if you'll be eating in or not. I don't cook dinner, not midday, unless it's a holiday, and then I don't cook supper.'

She turned to look at him. Good-looking boy, big and well put together. Reminded her a little of some good times she'd had thirty, forty years ago in Memphis, when the white gentlemen spent a lot of time in Hog Ridge looking for their dark and illicit pleasures.

He nodded. 'Ten bucks a week?' he said.

'That's right, and a week in advance to start. Twenty to move in, all told.'

He reached for his wallet. Her memory wasn't what it had been, and his name had gone clean out of her head. But she didn't want to embarrass herself, and so she said, 'How'd you pronounce that name again?'

He grinned, a rather spacey, almost manic expression, and she wondered if he was one of those drug addicts. But he looked clean enough, and though his hair was a little over his ears and down his neck, it wasn't one of those godawful girlish hippy styles. In fact, it looked as if it had been freshly cut and besides, she thought a lot of this addict stuff was overdone. She'd tasted a little of this and that, back in her Memphis days, and it hadn't seemed to do her any harm.

'Hm? Oh, they call me Mister Rosenweig,' he said.

'*Mister* Rosenweig? Well, fancy that.'

Francine Walters, a stick of a woman pushing six feet tall, with the features of a hound dog after a strong face lift, and an artfully arranged explosion of tinted and frosted blond hair, put on a pair of rubber gloves and began to rinse the shampoo out of Mabel McSorley's black hair. 'Lean back now, babe, and watch your eyes, OK?'

Mabel, the wife of Hank McSorley, who owned

146

the Cadillac-Buick-Chevy dealership out south on Oleander Drive, squinched her eyes a little tighter and said, 'What do you think, Francine? The roots are starting to show, aren't they? It's a damned crime, me barely past forty, and already the grey is everywhere.'

'I know, babe,' Francine replied as she squeezed a handful of shampoo bubbles out of Mabel's hair, and made no other reaction to this announcement of Mabel's age. Which she knew perfectly well was understated by at least ten years.

Francine knew that, like barbers and bartenders and others who tended to the personal needs of folks, there was a lot of art involved in the craft – and all three could pretty much nail the ages of their clients within a year or two. Skin, hair, nails, and drunks didn't lie, at least not very well. But as far as Francine was concerned, if Mabel McSorley wanted to pretend that she was going prematurely grey, Francine would personally be more than happy to charge her fourteen dollars plus a ten per cent tip for shampoo, cut, colour, once a month.

Besides, she liked Mabel, who could get a pretty raunchy mouth on her when the mood took. Which it seemed to be doing now. 'Fucking dimples,' Mabel remarked.

'What?' As far as Francine knew, and she was more than familiar with the territory, there was nothing resembling a dimple anywhere on Mabel's head. 'You ain't got any dimples, honey.'

'On my fucking knees,' Mabel said. Blindly, she waved one pudgy hand in the general direction of the offending joints. Francine lifted her head and took a look.

Mabel was one of those somewhat stout women who denied their stoutness by wearing clothes just a bit too tight, and just a bit too young. In this case, Mabel was wearing a pair of faded madras Bermuda shorts, the cuffs of which stuck out below the bottom of the green plastic bib protector tied around her neck. But lying back the way she was, it spread the soft flab of her thighs out, and they bulged against the hem of the shorts, blue varicose veins prominent against the pasty flesh. There were times Francine wished there was a law against shorts on women before the sun got hot enough to give a good tan.

'I see 'em,' she said. 'Dimples. Right in the middle of your knees. What you do, Mabel? Have your ankles lifted?'

Both women burst into delighted laughter at this. They were still chuckling as Francine whipped a big towel around Mabel's wet hair and led her back to the styling chair. 'I think you probably better get a colour, babe. This one won't hold for another month.'

Mabel sighed. 'Sometimes I feel like just cutting it all off. Though Hank would have a fit.'

'If that's what you decide, you come to me first. I'll use a straight razor on it, and you'll look like a bowling ball.'

Francine changed her gloves, did some colour mixing, and began to work the thick paste into Mabel's hair. 'Oh, say, hon, did you hear what the Preacher Buck's up to now?'

Mabel hadn't, and under normal circumstances wouldn't care much, since both she and Hank were pillars of the 'good' Methodist church, the Downtown High Street Methodist, not the AME over in Goat Town. But Mabel knew that in some dim way Preacher Buck carried on business with her husband beyond the new Caddy he bought every year.

'No, what's that?'

'Well, he wants to build a memorial to our boys. You know, local fellows went over to Veet-nam and died for their country? I guess there's two or three already, that Sydney Carpenter for one of them. I think he's gonna start a fund-raising drive or something.'

Mabel thought about it. Every day, it seemed like, she turned on the TV and saw these horrible pictures of brave American boys dying to save some worthless foreigners, and they didn't even appreciate it. Worse, right here at home the streets were full of filthy, long-haired degenerates spitting on, even *burning* the flag, calling police officers pigs, and, for all she knew, fucking in the

149

gutters. Although the last idea was not entirely unattractive.

But as for the rest, Mabel McSorley was pretty well fed up with it, and if Preacher Buck wanted to build a little monument for the side of good and light, then she was all for it. Unless, of course, Hank was against, but she doubted he would be. In fact, knowing Hank, he'd probably end up running the businessman's part of the fund drive.

'I think that's a fine idea, Francine. Is he taking donations yet?'

'I dunno . . .' Francine replied. Her chat with Thelma Ritter hadn't included any of the nuts and bolts.

'Well, I'll give him a call if I remember. And I'll mention it at the garden club tomorrow.'

Francine nodded in satisfaction, both with the condition of the dye on Mabel's scalp – it looked as if it was going to take – and with the results of the conversation. It looked as if *that* would take, too.

She patted Mabel on one shoulder. 'Say, hon, that's a good idea, too.'

'I know,' Mabel replied complacently. 'I hate those fucking hippies.'

By eight that night the weather had turned to what Lucas thought of as 'mixed', with a sharp wind blowing in from the northeast. He bet that if he drove out to the ocean he'd see some pretty cold whitecaps, though the tulips were almost past full bloom and the peonies were well into it. Didn't feel like rain, though there might be some fog later, he decided.

He pulled the GTO over to the curb in front of the parsonage, got out and locked the door. Mixed weather was no good to have the top down, and he didn't, though he didn't like the mouldy canvas smell that filled the car when he had it up.

He paused on the sidewalk outside the picket fence that guarded his father's flower beds and stood a moment, hands in the hip pockets of his jeans, and stared at the sky against which the cozy, lighted shape of the parsonage was framed. Looked like some old horror movie, he thought. The sky aboil with scudding dark clouds, the wind rising, the pines bent over at their tops like old Chinese men in pointed hats kowtowing, and the house, every window lit, curled like a fat tabby cat beneath all the evils of the night.

He snorted at this sudden, unlikely wash of melodrama. Next thing, he'd be talking to himself about vampires and werewolves. When it was only Daddy, and not the same thing at all. A talk of grave importance? He could just bet.

The gate opened smoothly when he nudged it with the toe of his cowboy boot. He stepped through, turned to watch it swing shut, then ambled on up the concrete walk as if he didn't have a care in the world.

The boards of the front porch creaked softly under his feet, and on his left the swing, painted fresh white and hanging from new chains, uttered vague, oily screeches as the wind pushed it back and forth. For a moment it was almost possible to imagine something invisible sitting there, rocking itself slowly in the gloom.

Lucas reached for the front door knob and turned it, but nothing happened. The door was locked. Odd. He couldn't ever remember the Preacher locking his door when he was at home.

To the left of the door, set into the frame, was a small round lighted button about the size of a nickel. He moved his finger towards it and jerked it back when a tiny spark leaped the three inches between the button and his fingertip.

'You quit that now, Daddy,' he murmured, mildly irritated. He just didn't see the need for all this mystery, for this childish fun and games the Preacher liked to engage in. Why couldn't he just come out and say what he had on his mind?

Lucas's lips thinned out and he mashed the button down. This time there was no spark, only a muffled *bing-bong* deep in the bowels of the house, each time he pressed the button.

'*Around the back . . .*' a thin voice called.

'What?'

'*I'm out back in the yard, Lucas, come on around!*'

Must be a trick of the wind, Lucas thought, to make his daddy's normally deep, carrying voice sound so thin and distant. The back yard wasn't that far away, after all.

He turned around, stepped off the porch, and walked around the side of the house. Dew sparkled on the grass and darkened the worn leather of his boots. The smell of the peonies planted in neat rows along the foundation bloomed up into his nose, the perfume so strong it was almost sickening – like the overwhelming, decayed sweetness of lilies in a cramped funeral parlour.

'You up on the porch, Daddy?' he called as he came around the back corner of the house.

'I'm down here, Lucas. Out by the back fence.'

Lucas peered down the murky lanes between the fruit trees, most of which had finally shed their loads of blossoms which now rotted on the shadowed earth beneath their skeletal limbs. He could barely make out his father's bulky, stolid shape at the far end of the orchard, faintly outlined by the intermittent moonlight. More fun and games. He felt his own irritation poke him like a thorn, and told himself, *That's what he wants, don't let him get ahead of you.*

Suddenly the wind reached down at him and scratched his skin, leaving a bumper crop of crawling gooseflesh behind. Lucas felt something catch in his throat, but he shook himself and called, 'Here I come, Daddy. Ready or not.'

'Oh, I'm ready, Lucas. You come on down and find out how much.'

Behind the Preacher something in the twisted green murk of the graveyard had begun to glow. The word Lucas had been trying to find all day suddenly came to his lips.

Witchy. Not a ghostly light. It was a *witchlight*.

Melanie Hankings stood peering out the window of her tiny room at the shadows slowly settling over Goat Town. Her part of town was considered ugly, but in the softness of a late Trinity spring, gilded by the sunset light, it was almost beautiful. She hugged herself and sighed. No use hiding in here much longer. Gage was still out there, and Lucas Buck, but she couldn't allow the fact they were there make her a prisoner here. No way, Jay.

She shook her head. Three days were enough to mourn her lost whatever it was. Virginity? Seemed a pompous term for something taken so casually and painfully. If it was so valuable, why could men take it so easily?

She examined this gloomy thought as if it were a particularly repellent root, plucked from rotten soil, but she could glean nothing from it. Maybe it was just the way the world was, and women had been getting the short end of the whipping stick since the very beginning of it.

I won't hide, she thought suddenly. *I will not hide.*

She stepped back from the window and

shinnied out of the slip which was all she'd worn the past three days. A clean T-shirt with no bra – to hell with the gossipy old biddies – and a worn pair of jeans. As she touched the soft grey-blue denim, a picture of another pair, with the zipper ripped out of the front, flashed on her mental screen. She turned that programme right off, though. She'd cut those jeans up with a razor blade and fed the shreds, handful by handful, down the toilet. Lucky she hadn't stopped the damned thing up.

She finished dressing, thought about makeup and then thought, the hell with it. Only a little walk around the neighbourhood, no reason to put on warpaint for that.

She slung the red canvas backpack she was using for a purse over her right shoulder by a single strap, and headed down the stairs. She'd hoped to avoid any maternal conversation, but the unavoidable rubbery scritch of her sneaker soles on the stair treads awakened Heppy from her slumber in front of the TV.

'Mellie, that you?'

'Yes, Mama.'

'You goin' out?'

'Just for a little walk. Got to feeling restless.'

'Come in here, let me look at you.'

Reluctantly, Melanie came around the bottom of the stairs and stood in the door to the front parlour.

'Mph. Well, you look a little better. You decided

yet to tell your mama what happened to you the other night?'

'Mama, I told you, nothin' happened.'

Heppy stared at her, her eyes dark and glittering. Her gaze made Melanie think about the crows that roosted on the telephone lines and watched everything with bright, piercing attention.

'Well,' Heppy said at last, 'I suppose you think you know best, and your mama don't know anything.'

'Mama . . .'

'Oh, go on, out with you, Mellie. Take your walk, it'll do you good, maybe.'

Gratefully, Melanie nodded, blew Heppy a kiss, and scooted out the door. It banged shut behind her, and Heppy listened to the footsteps of her youngest daughter hurry down the path. She knew too much, she thought. Things weren't right with Christine, either. Were all the Hankings women doomed to unhappiness?

Sometimes she thought that, in Trinity, they just might be.

Melanie reached the edge of her yard, stepped out onto the heaved and buckling slabs of the old sidewalk, where oak tree roots thrust right through the concrete. Turning left, she walked along for a while, crossing Washington and Jackson, till she came to Main, and turned left again. Up ahead, on her right, she saw the brown shutters and white trim of Ethel Bates's boarding house looming out of the dusk. She almost crossed the street to avoid walking past, because the porch there this time of the evening was often full of Miz Bates's factory men boarders, drinking Pearl and whistling and making comments about any woman foolish enough to walk by.

But what had she told herself not more than ten minutes ago? *I will not hide.*

She stuck her chin out and her head up. Let them think she was snooty if they wanted to. She didn't owe any of them one damn thing.

But she didn't look directly at the figures propped up there, leaning on the railing or sitting with their feet up, except to note out of the corner of her eye they were there, watching her. It was a creepy feeling. It made her wonder what those women who did stripteases felt like.

She was almost all the way past, and feeling the tension in her shoulders let go just a little bit, when somebody called out: 'Mellie? Is that you? Wait up!'

She turned. 'Larry . . . ?'

Chapter Nine

'It is called, in the old tongue, *ignis fatuus*,' the Preacher said, and made a spreading gesture with his right hand. 'Down here we call it will-o'-the-wisp, or friar's lantern. I like that, friar's lantern. I'm a friar, I guess, and you could say this lights my way.'

'Uh huh, Daddy, and we could call it swamp fire, or glow-worm, or late for dinner, for all I care. And if that's what you brought me out here to talk about, I think I'll just head on back home, thanks just the same.'

'Boy, you shut your mouth now.'

The two men stood next to the ancient, obscenely bulging boulder. All around them lurched the light; the stony earth bubbled with it, rank, corrupt, green and yellow, the colour of decomposing corpses, the slimy glimmer of rot and decay.

The two enigmatic tombstones glowed with a different hue, a frighteningly livid pink, the colour you got if you shone a flashlight through a strip of flesh, newly torn from living bone. Lucas stared at them, then turned back to his father.

'Daddy, fuck your ghost show. I'm not interested.'

Ghastly shadows played across the Preacher's heavy features; his eyes seemed sunken and yet fevered, and his skin looked stretched too tight, almost translucent, revealing the strings of muscle and tendon beneath the surface, and beneath that, the naked, staring skull.

'Lucas, your mama is buried here. Did you know that?'

Lucas paused. 'Nothing would surprise me, Daddy. Nothing about you, or this place. But I told you once. This is your place, not mine. I don't want it. You bought it, you pay for it, you keep it.'

He took a deep breath and stepped closer to his father. '*It's your deal, goddamn it!*'

But there was the faintest crack of uncertainty in his impromptu curse, and his father pounced on that as surely as any born predator. 'No, Lucas,' he replied, his voice a whisper. 'It's family, and it's yours, too; and someday it will be *only* yours. It's in your blood. And you *know* it.'

'No, Daddy. No. I didn't make the deal, and I won't keep it for your sake.'

'Yes you will, son. You've already taken it, grabbed on to it with both hands. You think I don't know?' The Preacher turned slowly, his burning eyes taking in the ancient devastation, the dead-lights centuries old.

'How it is?' he went on. 'How you just *know* things, how you think on something and *lo*! It happens? How you can just accidentally always *be* in the place you need to be, when you need to be there? That's part of the deal, Lucas. You take it willingly enough. Do you want to turn it down now?'

He chuckled as Lucas turned away. He reached out, grabbed Lucas's shoulder and spun him around. Lucas came with his hand up, curling into a fist, and his father laughed in his face.

'Go ahead! Strike me! Kill me, son, if you think you can!'

The skin of Lucas's face was stretched backward across his skull bones, as if some invisible wind was blowing against him, some inferno breath that threatened to peel the flesh right off. His teeth were exposed in an involuntary rictus; their white ridges caught the dreadful phosphorescence and echoed it, so that for a moment his mouth was filled with fiery fangs.

His balled fist began to quiver, then to shake. Ahhh!' he finally spat, as his chest heaved and his back jerked in unwitting spasms.

Suddenly he bent over, put his palms to his knees and held there, gasping, as if he'd just run ten miles without a breath. Sweat covered his forehead and dripped off the tip of his nose. He shook his head, and glittering drops flew from his soaked hair.

'Submit, Lucas,' his father said.

He didn't look up. 'No, Daddy.'

'Submit!'

'No. Never.'

Overhead the clouds began to whirl and coalesce around the bilious moon. Lucas glanced up. That moon was full as ever, though it should be on the wane now. But it wasn't, and now it vomited its own sickly yellow contribution to the miasmic light that polluted the graveyard. It came to him then: the moon was always full here.

He stared for a long moment, feeling the thin skin of real things stretching beyond their natural boundaries, feeling the chill of the beyond seeping slowly across the torn barrier, the entry, the opening, the door—

Here.

The horror.

It took the last of his strength, but he stood upright. He looked at his father, and after a time he unfolded a smile like a new switchblade.

'I renounce, Daddy,' he whispered.

His father recoiled as if struck, his mouth forming a dark oh! of shock. 'No . . .'

'I do, Daddy. Take your deal back. This is yours. I don't want it, you understand? On the bones of my mother, I *renounce* it.'

The Preacher staggered, and placed the flat of his hand on top of the boulder for support. Dark and twisted fire seemed to run up his arm then, and spread as a ravening metastasis until his whole shape was limned in the grisly fluorescence of the pit.

'You will be alone . . .' the Preacher intoned, as if pronouncing a formal curse. But Lucas's smile never wavered, not for an instant, in that febrile darklight.

'But Daddy, didn't you know? I have been, every minute of my life.'

Then he turned and made his way out of the hellish mire, folding his Gordian knife of a smile away, and listening not at all to the shriek that rose in his wake.

'You *renounce*? No, spawn of mine, *I renounce you!*'

He knew it was a curse, and he didn't care. He would make his own deals now, for he was free of the unholy pacts his ancestors had made – and kept. There was a fierce joy to that, to the uncertainty of being utterly dependent on himself alone.

He wondered how that would work, and if he would get a chance to find out. Or if the inhuman things in the graveyard would find a way to kill him first: and maybe his daddy most of all. It was no accident of history, he understood, that Buck men tended to die ugly – and young.

In the way of small towns everywhere, it spread fast. Hank McSorley did take up the banner, and made an extemporaneous speech to three of his peers at the same table that the ladies of the auxiliary frequented in the Elks restaurant.

'Now, listen here, Cam. I know you don't go in much for charity, but what the hell, this is more like politics, really. We need your help. I need it, the town needs it. I talked with old Buck, and then I did some research. We can put us up a nice little monument for, oh, twenty grand or so. But it ain't the money, you know, although I expect you to dig deep into that wrinkled old wallet of yours.'

Cambridge 'Cam' Palkington, a longtime stalwart of the county Democratic organization and senior sitting member of the town council, rubbed the thick vein that wandered over the top of his bald skull before he replied. Hank McSorley thought this was a good sign. Every time Cam rubbed himself like that, it meant he was getting ready to go for it. Hank had made a fair amount of money over the years with that scrap of knowledge, sitting in the room beyond the back door of this very restaurant, in the card room of the club. Cam hadn't caught on, for Hank guarded his advantage jealously, and only used it when Cam started to double up his bets in their Saturday night poker games.

'Ah, hell, maybe you got something, Hank. I dunno, though, it sounds like supporting that bastard Nixon, and you know I hate that.'

Phil Lanier, who owned all three of the Texaco

stations in town, said, 'It's a good thing, Cam. The world is changing too fast, and not for the better, either. All these goddamned revolutionaries, turning our kids' heads and filling them with Commie lies. Ain't nothing sacred anymore. We got to make a stand somewhere. And this is as good a place as any, I guess.'

'A lot of the church men hereabouts aren't gonna go along with Preacher Buck, you know,' Cam said.

Hank nodded. 'All the more reason to back him up. Some of these reverends—' he cocked one eyebrow at Father Jim Dalford, sipping his customary noonday martini at a table with two of the stalwarts of the Knights of Columbus three tables over '—well, you got to wonder if they really believe in the United States of America, or if they answer to some pack of foreigners that don't give a hoot about us at all.'

In Trinity, at least in certain circles, the great battle over JFK and just who that martyred president answered to, ultimately, was still being fought with the same bitterness as the War of the Secession.

'And some of the schoolteachers, too,' added Nelson DeMille, owner of DeMille's Hardware.

'Don't I know it,' Hank said. 'Between the churches and the schools, our kids ain't got half a chance of growing up to be decent Americans. All I'm saying is we got a chance to stand up for something we believe in. What do you say, then? Is it worth some of your time and money?'

Hank looked around the table, taking care to catch each of their eyes in turn. He felt that good, warm, solid feeling he always got when he knew somebody was just about to put their name on the dotted line for a new Buick. It was a God-given talent he had, to be able to close a deal like this.

And if his oldest son, Jamie (who would have hair down to his ass right now if Hank wasn't still big enough to take the boy out to the back yard and whip his snotnose young ass), even if Jamie was likely to be carrying a sign saying his daddy was a war criminal, well, hell. Every family has its little ups and downs.

Yes, there was such a thing as freedom of speech, Hank supposed, even if he didn't like it when that knife cut so close to the bone. But it seemed to him that all these damned protestors and agitators were only concerned with the freedom part, and none of the responsibility.

'I'm in,' Cam said finally. The other two nodded and grunted. 'Good enough,' Hank said. 'I'll count on each of you for a cheque, then. Say five hundred?'

Nelson DeMille winced, and Hank understood, because the hardware business hadn't been so good lately. Nels hadn't even traded in his Oldsmobile this year, though up until recently it had been an annual ritual with him. But even

Nelson finally opened up his sportcoat and flopped a battered chequebook down on the table top.

'That's good, boys. That's real good,' Hank McSorley said. 'Make the cheques out to Reverend Buck. He's got an account opened at the Merchant's National.'

He paused, then grinned slowly. What the hell, he was on a roll. Might as well go for the big kill. 'Did I mention that a thousand will get your name on the bronze plaque as a benefactor?'

'Larry, I think you're crazy,' Melanie told him, but Larry only laughed. They were sitting together on the porch of Ethel Bates's boarding house, which at this time of a Tuesday afternoon was usually deserted. Ethel's boarders tended to be either working men or drinking men, and the weekday afternoons saw little of either variety.

Melanie wasn't sure she liked this new version of Larry Rosenweig that had returned so unexpectedly to Trinity, though she did sense an element of welcome inevitability. But his moods were different than before. They swung, a little bit too much for comfort, between giggling, manic highs and introspective, muttering lows. When he was down he was awfully hard to be around, but when he was high, he was more than a little scary. His eyes would glitter, and once, when he was

166

talking about Lucas Buck, a thin line of spit began to leak from the corner of his mouth and he didn't even seem to notice.

Which was another worry. Lucas had run his ass out of town, or at least he'd thought he had. What would he do if he found Larry had come back? Larry might think he was more than a match for 'that fucking peckerwood', as he had taken to calling Lucas now, but Melanie had her doubts. Had big doubts, in fact, not only about the possible results of Larry's under-estimation of Lucas, but about her own feelings on the same subject.

She had made sure to avoid Lucas Buck ever since the night out at the river. She wasn't quite sure why – Lucas had been nothing but a gentleman when he'd dropped her off at her house – but she sensed something else there. Some potential she wasn't sure she wished to acknowledge, as if by doing so she might accept some deal between the two of them whose implications she didn't fully understand.

Nor had Lucas made any effort to press the issue. She'd seen him driving around with his friends, mostly Ben Healy, but that was all. She was pretty sure he'd seen her, too, but he hadn't tried to speak or anything.

As far as Gage Temple went, she hadn't seen him at all. So Larry, unexpected as he was, was for the moment the only game in town. Unless she wanted to spend the summer sitting at home, caught in the baleful gaze of Heppy and Josh's judgemental ignorance.

'There's boys dying in Vietnam for nothing but fascism,' Larry said earnestly. 'Nothing more than the Nazis in Washington and the greedy capitalists that sell guns to everybody.'

She rubbed the toe of one sneaker on the other and said, 'You sound like a speech, Larry. Like that McGovern fellow.'

'He's going to beat Nixon, you know,' Larry replied. 'It doesn't look good now, but you can't fool all the people all of the time. Nixon's a crook, Mellie. Of course he's no different than a lot of them, Democrats and Republicans both. Down around here, there isn't a dime's worth of difference between them anyway.'

She glanced towards the cool shadows floating behind the big open doors off the porch. 'You want to be careful with what you say, Larry. You never know who might be listening in.'

But Larry's face had taken on that stretched shine, and his eyes seemed faintly bulging. 'I don't care, Mellie. If we don't speak up, who will? It's our duty. This damned Vietnam memorial, you know? It's a crime.'

She shrugged. 'Don't see what's so bad about it. They got other ones in the park, too.'

But he shook his head slowly, with the spurious patience of someone instructing a student whose intelligence was slightly suspect. 'No, Mellie. Do you see any monuments to the Nazis? Even in Germany? Well, this is the same thing. They want to put up a monument to baby killers who are no better than the Nazis were. That's what I'm telling you.'

She considered for a long moment. When he put it that way – and his eyes got so dark and interesting and she could smell the aroma of sweat and dedication baking off him – the idea held a certain logical attraction. Or he did. She wasn't exactly sure which of the two it was. Maybe both. And a part of her wanted to find out. It wasn't as if she had anything to lose any more, like her virginity.

'All right, Larry, what do you want me to do?'

'There's kids at the high school that would help, aren't there?'

She nodded. 'A few. Maybe more than a few.'

'Well, good, then. We need to get them organized.'

'How you gonna do something like that?'

'Well, the first thing is to get them together, and I've got an idea or two that might work. What I need for you to do is . . .'

She sat, one elbow propped on her knee, nodding and listening, and wondered if Larry could get over the sound of his voice long enough to walk out to the river with her later on.

*   *   *

'Marvis,' Gage Temple said, 'you still talk to all them stump-pullin' Klucker kin of yours, back in the piney woods?'

'Well, sure, Gage. Where you think I get this shine from? The Ace Liquor store?'

Gage mulled that over, then spat a glistening wad over the porch railing of his tumbledown house. It landed on the dry brown dust of his front yard and made a moist black spot. He eyed it for a moment, then went on: 'Well, any of them had something to say about this Veet-nam memorial thing?'

'What Veet-nam memorial, Gage?'

Gage eyed him. 'Don't you pay no attention to public affairs, Marvis? Hell, it's all over town by now.' Which indeed it was, though Gage had a little more efficient pipeline into the news of the day than most people did.

Marvis shrugged. All over town didn't mean much to him. If it was being talked about at the bar or the pool tables at the Country House Pub, he might take note, but civic responsibility wasn't his strongest suit. Truth be told, he had a bum knee and a 4-F draft classification, and didn't give that much of a ratfuck about Veet-nam at all.

Anyway, the subject bored him. 'You think we got enough lightning there to last the weekend, Gage?' It was a fair question; ever since he'd gone and found Gage out by the river with a knot the size of a softball on the side of his head and a set of stove-in ribs, Gage had been . . . well, strange. Just laid up around that old house of his, not doing a thing but sucking down corn.

Marvis, who normally would have thought that was the life of Riley, was beginning to get a little worried. Gage was putting away a couple of jars a day, and given that this shine was the real deal, almost pure alcohol, that wasn't quite human. But the more Gage drank, the more he wanted, and it didn't seem to be affecting him much. Except for his temper, of course, which had been purely miserable ever since that night out by the river. Marvis would have given a pretty penny to find out the truth of that story.

Gage leaned back on the orange crate he'd dragged to the front of the porch and cocked one eye at the cardboard box near the top of the steps. 'Got eight jars there . . . well, counting the one we're on right now.' He belched thoughtfully. 'That should do her, I guess. Unless you get a lot more thirsty than usual, Marvis.'

Then he laughed suddenly, and the sound of that unsettled Marvis even more than Gage's sour temper of late.

'They had a meeting in the park a couple of days ago,' Gage said.

Marvis shook his head. That one had gone right by him. 'Who did, Gage?'

'Them fucking Commies is who. Protestors, whatever you want to call them. Musta been twenty or thirty of them, and some guy from up north, some Yankee whaddayacallit, an agitator, stirrin' them all up about that monument the Preacher wants to build.'

Marvis stared at him wide-eyed. 'Commies? Right here in Trinity? Surely that ain't right, Gage.'

Gage rubbed his belly where it bulged out beneath his grease-streaked T-shirt. His ribs were still strapped up tight with adhesive tape, and it itched like the devil.

'Well, a lot of them are just high school kids, and some teachers and preachers and shit. Not all that many, but more than we need, you know what I'm sayin'?'

Marvis nodded slowly. 'What are you saying, Gage?'

'We got to do something. And I figger all those bedsheet Klucker relatives of yours are just the thing we need.'

Marvis thought that the backwoods members of the Pickney clan, the ones who kept their white robes and pointy hats freshly laundered and ready to go, were, if anything, even less useful than he was. But if Gage thought different, it was fine with him. Cousin Earl Pickney and his brood of eight boys weren't all that hard to find, anyway. Not if you knew where to look.

He was considering this as another thought wandered, unbidden, into his internal conversation and turned the key to his jaw.

'Gage, you see anything of Mellie Hankings lately?'

'She was at the meeting in the park.' Gage hitched himself closer to the railing, his eyes now glassy and distant. 'And you know who else was there? Lucas Buck. Now don't that beat everything?'

Marvis nodded. 'Sure does, Gage.'

Gage squinted up at the sky. 'I don't like Lucas anymore, you know,' he said softly.

It was a harmless enough thing to say, but for some reason, even in the summer heat, Marvis shivered.

Preacher Buck hung up the phone, a satisfied expression smoothing his heavy features. Hank McSorley was doing yeoman's work on the memorial project. He'd pretty much taken over the day-to-day organizing, and was doing a fine job of it, too. Something would have to be done for him, something nice. The Preacher leaned back in his squeaky old wooden armchair and considered a moment. Nothing came immediately to mind, but he'd think of something. That was the way of the world. You made your deals and paid your debts, and one hand shook the other.

He thought about that as he watched motes of dust dance in the light through the cabbage-rose chintz curtains. Too bad Lucas didn't understand that. But that wasn't really it, was it?

Lucas *did* understand. He just wouldn't accept. Well, the blood was still the blood, and there wasn't a thing he could do about that. Oh, he could fight it – in a way, the Reverend supposed, fighting it was a part of growing up to it. Accepting it.

When you're young, the hard way is the only way you ever learn anything. He sighed and closed his eyes. Lucas hadn't called or come by since that night in the graveyard. But he was still out and about, as if nothing had happened. In his mind's eye, the Preacher could see Lucas's red GTO right now, parked in front of Ethel Bates's boarding house, over in Goat Town. And wasn't that an interesting little meeting? Surely Lucas, in his desperation, had not sunk to this?

In a way it was plain ridiculous. If Lucas thought he was going to break the chains of obligation and blood with the likes of Mellie Hankings or some no-name Yankee boy, he would find out just how wrong a man could be. And that was the point, wasn't it? To teach him that lesson.

Submit!

And if he thought to make the choice between blood and Mellie, the Reverend thought, why, I'll take that one any day of the week. He chuckled and wondered how Lucas liked being just like plain folks for the first time in his life. There was one problem, though: ever since the night in the graveyard, he could still see Lucas when he

174

wanted to, but he didn't seem to be able to know him anymore. With the breaking of the connection, the ability to understand was also shattered.

Lucas was up to something, all right. And it would come clear eventually. It always did. If Lucas had a different idea of things, he would find out the truth, soon enough. And that truth, the Reverend reflected, was much as the philosopher Hobbes had said it was, for men who chose to live without other security than what their own strength and invention could furnish: they could expect lives solitary, poor, nasty, brutish, and short.

That was a big mouthful to swallow, and Preacher Buck expected Lucas might choke on it a bit as it went down. But swallow it he would, of that the Preacher had no doubts at all.

Chapter Ten

Larry checked his watch again, wondering if Mellie would come by. It had been a long and productive day, and when she'd finally headed for home, she'd said she was going to bed. Alone, she'd added with a smile. But he felt things coming together between them, in some indefinable but pleasant way, and if she was feeling the same things, maybe she'd change her mind. He sure wouldn't turn her down, if she did.

He put his boots up on Miz Bates's railing, and tilted his face towards the sky. There was something about these southern heavens, he couldn't quite put his finger on it, but they were different than the nights in Indiana. Softer, somehow, more comforting. Or maybe it was just the weather, melting and humid, that sort of leached things out of you. He thought if that was true, it might explain a lot about things down here. Maybe the parts he hated weren't actively evil, but more a passive kind of moral laziness: big wheel turning, too hot to worry, just let it go. That kind of thing.

He was going to shake them up anyway. Yeah, and that was the fucking truth of it – these people were stuck in a world a hundred years dead, a place where the Confederate flag still waved. An abominable world. A world not ready for Mister Rosenweig, but going to get him anyway.

So he mused, as the horned moon floated higher, and the old grandfather clock in Ethel Bates's foyer made a quiet little winding sound, then began to bong out the hour of eleven. He was half in a doze, caught between his pleasant dreams and the silky night, when the GTO idled to the curb and stopped.

Larry dropped his feet to the floor and leaned forward in his rocker. A nasty electric shiver contracted the muscles between his shoulder blades as he watched a shadowy figure step out of the car and pause. Looking up at him.

'That you, Larry?' Lucas Buck called softly.

'What do you want?' Larry licked his lips and felt his fingernails dig into his palms as he balled his fists. Just keep on thinking it. Mister Rosenweig, they call me *Mister* Rosenweig.

'Just to talk. That's all, nothing else.'

Larry waited a count of five, to see if Buck would say anything more, but he didn't. He just stood there, waiting in the dark, silent.

'Come on up, then,' Larry said. With an effort of will, he forced his hands to uncurl. As Lucas stepped up onto the concrete walk, his boots made soft scraping sounds.

Larry went to meet him at the top of the steps. Lucas paused below him, looking up. 'You going to let me up there, or should we just talk like this? All the same to me.'

In the faint light of the yellow bug lamp in the porch ceiling, Lucas's shadowed features looked relaxed and inoffensive. Larry wanted to feel there was something wrong here, but he couldn't find the edge of anger he needed. Even when he thought about what Lucas had done to him out on the road beyond the bridge, it somehow seemed long ago. Far away. He shrugged and stepped aside, never realizing just how much his mood had changed in a few brief moments.

'So. Pull up a chair. It's a free porch, I guess.'

Lucas grinned and hitched his rear onto the porch railing. Larry took back his rocker, then noticed he had to look up at Lucas. He climbed back to his feet, looked around, then went to the corner of the porch and grabbed a piece of the railing for himself. Now, the two of them being much the same size, they were on eye level. Larry thought it felt a lot better than looking up at the sonofabitch.

They sat like that, Lucas swinging one leg idly back and forth, and listened to the sound of the crickets, and a few frogs ratcheting away in Miz Bates's back yard. After a while, Lucas said, 'We didn't get off to a very good start, Larry. I feel bad about that, and I came over to apologize.'

For the first time in his life, Larry thought he might understand the meaning of the word flabbergasted. He opened his mouth, shut it, opened it again. 'Uh . . . well.'

Now Lucas grinned. 'Hey, I know what it must sound like. And hell, Larry, there isn't any reason for you to think anything good about me. But I was wrong.' He shrugged. 'That's it, I guess. All I had to say. So I guess I'll be on my way. You have a nice evening now, Larry.'

He slid off the railing and turned for the steps. Larry said, 'I saw you.'

'What's that?'

'I saw you at the rally we had. You were kind of mixing in at the back, out of the way, but I saw you. It's your father that's pushing this damned Vietnam memorial. Are you out here spying or something?'

Lucas laughed softly. 'No, I'm not spying, not now, and not at that rally, either. I don't expect you to understand, but my daddy and I don't agree on every little thing. How about you? You and your daddy always on exactly the same page?'

Something about the way he said it made Larry see Milton then, as sharply and clearly as he'd ever seen his father in his own mind. Good old Milton, smiling and sweating and pretending that it didn't make any difference he had to build his house *across* the street from Brentwood Estates.

He shook his head. 'No, we don't agree on everything.'

Lucas nodded. 'Lot of that going around, I guess. Even in redneck pisspot towns like Trinity.'

Larry felt a fresh wave of surprise. A couple of minutes ago he'd thought he was going to have to fight, and now this guy was saying almost exactly what Larry had been thinking all along.

And Lucas grinned as if he could read Larry's mind. 'You think just because this town is like it is, everybody in it is blind. But hell, boy, we're like anywhere else. We even got our own hippies. This little crusade of yours, it's got a lot more support than you might expect. Did you know that?'

Dumbly, Larry shook his head. 'Why are you telling me this?'

'I don't know. Cause I felt like it, I guess. And maybe I want to help.'

'Help?' Larry stood up off the railing. The movement made him faintly dizzy. The inner map of his current world, so carefully drawn, was in tatters. 'Well, I guess we can use all the help we can get.'

'I figured,' Lucas said. He turned around, squatted down and settled himself on the top step, looking out at the empty street. A hoot owl uttered its eerie cry, and down the block, a dog began to bark.

'Here's one piece right now,' he went on. 'I see

you're keeping yourself pretty well in the background, letting Mellie do the upfront talking.'

Larry came up behind him, hesitated, then sat down next to him. 'It seemed better. Folks around here, they like to talk about outside agitators a lot. I figured, why give them the target?'

'Yeah, that's the way I guessed it was. But listen, Larry, you want to watch yourself anyhow. What you're doing, it's got some folks stirred up that you need to be careful of.'

'Like who?'

'You know anything about the Kluckers?'

'The what?'

'Kluckers. You know – oh, maybe you wouldn't. The Klan, the KKK. The bedsheet boys. We still got 'em, though nobody much likes to advertise the fact.'

Larry felt his old antagonism come flooding back. 'So what are you telling me? That I should back off, or the fucking Klan is gonna come after me? Is this my official warning or something?'

But Lucas only raised one hand, held it, then let it fall back. 'No, that's not what I'm saying at all. You go on, but keep an eye over your shoulder. They're cowards for the most part, but that don't mean they won't hurt you. People think bullies will back down if you face them, but it isn't true. Bullies are the way they are because they *like* to hurt you. And they tend to be good at it, know what I mean?'

Larry felt the closeness Lucas seemed to exude by his mere physical nearness. Larry knew he ought to be feeling a lot more wary than he did, but there was something comfortable about Lucas. Ridiculous as that might seem. He exhaled slowly. 'Well, then, thanks for the warning. I'll take your advice.'

'Oh, there's more. I know a good deal about what goes on in this town. And if I hear of anything starting to happen, I'll let you know. How about that? A deal?'

'You offered me a deal before, remember? I didn't think it was a very good one. And since we're both sitting here talking, I guess you know I didn't take you up on it.'

'Oh, hell, Larry, I already apologized for that. I was being an asshole, pure and simple. No, this is straightforward. I'll look after you as well as I can, and all you need to do is remember that I'm your friend. That's it, OK?'

There still seemed to be something thick and narcotic in the night air, but turn it as he would, Larry couldn't find the thorn in Lucas's bouquet. He leaned back and stretched. Amazing how relaxed he felt, all of a sudden.

'OK, Lucas. I'll keep that in mind.'

'Shake on it?'

Larry took his hand. 'Deal,' he said.

*   *   *

LaVelle Baker walked along Harbutton Lane, heading away from the town square. He was bouncing a basketball back and forth with his best friend, Calvin Hendricks, while carrying on a running line of patter with Calvin about how white boys really couldn't play basketball, and Calvin was living proof of that idea. They had not paid much attention to the small groups of mostly fellow students, and a few adults, who were drifting away from the square after a rally opposing the Vietnam memorial, although an unknowing observer might have thought the two boys were a part of the general crowd.

LaVelle didn't care about any of that protest crap because he assumed that when he graduated from Trinity High, he would enlist. As a young black man, he didn't plan to stay in the south all his life, and the risk of his life against a college education bought and paid for by the GI Bill seemed fair enough to him. As for Calvin, he had already put in his preliminary application to Chapel Hill, where generations of Hendricks boys had got degrees. His grades were fine, and he anticipated no problems in avoiding military service for however long it took – he had more or less decided to become a lawyer, and he didn't think they would draft lawyers. Anyway, the draft board here in Trinity was made up of old fogeys who knew his family and, in some cases, owed individual members. His father and his father's brother had done very well over the years, and had collected tall stacks of IOUs along the way.

If either of the boys thought about the protestors at all, it was to wonder whether they had any decent pot for sale. Which was a thing both of them, in the way of kids, thought was pretty funny. Nobody would suspect them of toking on the demon weed – not with haircuts no longer than fingernails, and solid positions on the high school basketball second string, LaVelle even had hopes of being a starter come the fall season – but like everybody else they knew, they'd been known to smoke a little. What the hell, hemp grew wild along the rivers down here. You could go out and cut yourself down a stalk ten feet tall, even if it was so weak you had to smoke a bushel basket to get really high. But the only thing about either of them that betrayed this occasional lapse was the shirt Calvin was wearing – a tank top, what his daddy might have called a strappy-T, but this one had the red, white and blue pattern of the American flag – with a few white stars thrown in for good measure. His daddy had not liked that shirt much, but Calvin didn't mean any harm by it, since he didn't think of it as the flag, exactly, but more as a cool design.

The summer evening was still sweet; a few soft rags of breeze touched them. The muffled laughter of the hippie protestors – as they thought of them – sounded distant, yet comforting. Like lying in a hammock, snugly wrapped up, listening to the faraway grumble of a storm.

Neither of them noticed the battered, primer-grey Chevy van with one blind headlight that turned the corner behind them and slowed suddenly, the decal of the Confederate flag on its rear bumper catching the light from a passing street-lamp. And even if they had, they wouldn't have thought anything of it. Just some old boys from the backwoods, come into town for a beer or two, most likely down at the Country House Pub (which used to be called the White Way Café, but times had changed, even in Trinity). So they walked on, whipping the basketball back and forth, as the van crept up behind them like some stalking mechanical beast waiting for its chance to pounce.

Earl Pickney was sweating up a storm. The interior of the van, even with the two windows open, stank like the inside of a two-hole country shitter, what with three of his four oldest boys sprawled in the back, around a case of Dixie that was mostly done with. The air was thick with rancid, beery breath, ripe farts, and a haze of smoke from the Lucky Strikes everybody was smoking like chimneys.

Earl ground out his own Lucky in the over-flowing dashboard ashtray and peered through the streaked windshield. 'You see 'em?' he asked Earl Junior, who was sitting shotgun and trying to ignore his brothers, Purvis, Delano, and Eddie in the back.

Junior stuck his head out the window, squinted, and pulled back in. 'Them two boys? With the basketball? You reckon that's some of them?'

Earl shrugged. 'Got to be, I figure. They're walking along with all the rest of them, aren't they?'

'But they got short hair, Daddy. They don't look like no hippies to me.'

'Communists look like anything, I guess,' Earl said darkly. 'That white boy, look at his shirt. He's profanin' the American flag.'

Earl wasn't very strong on the actual meaning of the word profaning, but he knew his Communists. He'd brought a Purple Heart back from the Korean War – a jeep had rolled on him and broken his leg during a drunken midnight ride – and Communists truly scared the shit out of him. He'd been one of those who'd slogged through the winter in the long retreat from the Chosin Reservoir, and he would never forget his personal nightmare of little yellow men pouring out of the night like pus from a lanced boil, killing as they came. Of course there weren't any Communists here in Trinity, but as far as Earl was concerned, eternal vigilance was the ticket. If you didn't stop the Communists at the first sign, the next thing you knew, they'd be raping your women and pillaging the Seven Eleven stores.

Earl reached down between the seats and wrapped his hand around the taped handle of the sawed-off baseball bat there. 'You see anybody else, Junior?'

'Nope,' he said, after another quick look.

'OK,' Earl said. He eased down on the accelerator and crept ahead of Calvin and LaVelle, who glanced, incuriously, in his direction, then went back to their game. They were on Magnolia Way now, a quiet stretch with only one streetlight. The houses were set well back, and most of them were dark. 'Hey, you boys back there, get your shit together.'

He heard muffled movement, a thump, drunken giggles. 'Now you remember what I said. You just fling open the side doors, jump out, and take care of business when I give you the word. Me and Junior will be right behind you.'

Somebody – it sounded like Purvis – said, 'You say the word, Daddy.'

Earl nodded to himself as he guided the van to the curb about twenty yards up the street from Calvin and LaVelle and turned off the engine and lights. He didn't pay much attention to the goings-on in town, but he'd been genuinely shocked by what Marvis had told him about the Vietnam memorial and the protestors.

This wasn't official Klan business, but he would make it so if it came to it. No, tonight was just sort of a little how-de-do from the Pickney clan, speaking up for a better America.

Calvin and LaVelle drifted past. Calvin missed one of LaVelle's passes, scrabbled for the ball, corralled it and came up laughing. Earl thought it was a shame, in a way. They both looked like nice enough kids, except of course one was a nigger. But if they'd been bitten by the Communist bug, there was only one way to stop that in its tracks.

'OK, boys,' Earl said, gripping the baseball bat in one sweaty fist. 'Let's get to it.'

Georgina Hendricks was still shaken by it all. She stood looking out, down through the oaks at the silent street below, from her bedroom window on the second floor of the huge and empty-feeling Victorian house she'd inherited from her husband. It was so peaceful out there, so hard to believe what had happened on a similar street not three blocks away. As she thought about it, her hand began to quiver, rattling the half-melted ice cubes in her glass of Gilbey's gin. It was her fourth of the evening, two past her limit, but she didn't care. She needed something. It had been so horrible. Poor Calvin.

The call had come late last night, around eleven o'clock. Ted Hendricks, her brother-in-law, had called and said, 'Georgina, you better get down here to the hospital. Calvin's been hurt bad.'

Of course she'd gone right away. Calvin was her favourite nephew, a sweet boy who always remembered her birthday with a card and a hand-picked bouquet of wildflowers. She hadn't seen as much of him in recent years – he was growing up and, like a lot of Trinity's younger folks, perhaps beginning to grow away, as well – but she still remembered his cheerful grin when he'd sat in her kitchen as a young boy, washing down prodigious numbers of home made chocolate chip cookies with the two per cent milk his mother, Mary Ann, made him drink.

Now she winced as a different scene floated into her thoughts. She didn't want to see it anymore, but it wouldn't go away, not for long. She'd got down to the hospital ten minutes after the call, her hair already up in curlers for the night. Ted and Mary Ann were waiting. Ted's face was whiskery and grey and drawn; huge black bags had appeared under his bloodshot eyes. Mary Ann sat with her legs drawn up beneath her, on one of a pair of cheap chrome and vinyl chairs in the corner, her right hand fisted over her mouth, her eyes wide and hollow. She had on no makeup, and let out a sniff every once in a while.

'What happened?' she asked Ted.

He shook his head. 'We don't know. He was coming home from playing basketball with his friend LaVelle, and somebody attacked them. Beat them with baseball bats, the police say.'

Georgina gasped. 'Oh, my God. Is he – are they – all right?'

'No, Georgina, they aren't all right. Cal's got a fractured skull, broken ribs, his right arm broken in two places, and the doctors say internal injuries, too. He just got out of the operating room a few minutes ago.'

She let out her breath in a long, shuddery sigh. 'And the other boy?' She had met LaVelle a couple of times, and he seemed like a nice boy, too.

Ted stared at her for several beats, then shook his head. 'He didn't make it,' he said.

'Dear Lord . . .'

'Do you want to see him?' Ted asked. 'He's not awake, but you could look in.'

Georgina didn't want to look in, but she did, and now, almost twenty-four hours later, it was that picture she couldn't keep out of her mind for more than a few minutes at a time.

The room was lit only by one overhead fluorescent light that flickered and buzzed viciously, casting a hollow, clinical glare. The room stank of ether and disinfectant and, faintly, shit.

Calvin lay on a high hospital bed, with wires and tubes connected to machines and bags of blood and medicine. His face, below the thick bandage that covered his skull, was the same colour French's mustard gets if you leave it out to dry. His lips were swollen and split, marred with bloody black stitches. Another patchwork of sewing ran down from beneath the bandage all the way to his chin. Huge yellow-black bruises had swollen his eyes shut. His right arm, in a heavy cast, was elevated, and dangled limply from a contraption that reminded her of a hangman's gallows.

The room was full of a bubbly, liquid sound, and it took her a second to realize it was the sound of Calvin's breathing.

She'd looked for only a moment, and then had to turn away. He'd been a husky boy, she remembered, but now only a husk remained.

'Is he . . . ?'

Ted took her gently by the shoulders. 'They don't know yet, sis. Say it might be fifty-fifty. We're praying.' He nodded to himself. 'I want you to take Mary Ann home. Can you do that?'

Of course she could. But when she went over to her sister-in-law, Mary Ann looked up at her out of eyes like blind and bottomless wells and whispered, 'They say his brain is hurt, Georgina. His *brain* . . .'

She shivered and tossed back the rest of her gin.

'The police say it might have had something to do with the memorial. That those poor boys got mistaken for the protestors, or something. There'd been a rally just before, in the square, and everybody was still walking home.'

Georgina sighed and put down her empty glass. 'You know, I've been planning something for a while, and this is it. I hate this town – there's something sick here. Something rotten at its core, and I don't want anything to do with it anymore.'

She clenched her fist. 'I'm going to sell everything off. My husband's long dead, what would he care? I'm going to find a condo in Arizona, Phoenix, maybe. But I'm done here. As soon as we know for sure, one way or the other, about Calvin, then I'm leaving.'

Lucas Buck shifted on the sheets of her big maple bed, the back of his head propped against its carved headboard. The muscles of his naked chest moved smoothly in the shadowy light. She watched him and thought he might be the only thing about this accursed town she would miss when she was gone. But he wasn't enough to keep her, either. Nothing was, not any more.

Lucas nodded. 'I can't argue with you, Georgina. You got to do what you got to do. Sell everything off, though? That's a tall order, isn't it? Maybe you'd do better to keep it, and live off the income?'

'No! I don't want anything here to bring me back. You understand?'

He sighed. 'I guess I do, Georgina. You're determined?'

'I am.'

'It'll be hard, then, but I guess I can fix up something with my daddy. Take a lot of cash to swing a deal like that, and he's probably the only man in town with the means to get it done.'

She'd always known, through her husband and

his brother, that the Preacher was a bigger financial force in Trinity than most people reckoned, but this surprised her. She knew what her holdings were worth. She was not a stupid woman, nor financially ignorant. If the Reverend was going to take the whole bite himself, he'd better have a very big wallet. She wanted to leave – she would leave – but she'd get her price, first.

'Your father?' she murmured, as she lowered herself slowly into his arms.

'Uh huh,' Lucas said. 'We'll work out some kind of deal.'

'Mellie?'

The town square of Trinity was a gracious place under even ordinary conditions, but today, with the air sparkling in a limpid transparency that was different from anything Larry remembered back in Middletown, Indiana, it seemed about as perfect as any place could be. The grass was thick and green, its colour so vivid it almost hurt his eyes to look at it. And the ancient, noble oak trees that shaded the white-painted benches murmured as the wind played gentle songs through their leaves. All of which made the rest of it that much more horrible, like finding a big runny turd sitting on top of a wedding cake.

'Mellie, please. You can't do this.'

She was sitting next to him on one of the benches, not far from the one imperfection in that spreading lawn; the trampled spot near the Confederate memorial where they had held the rally two nights before.

'Larry, we can't go on with this. Don't you understand?' Her voice was low and ragged. She sounded very tired and, as she shook her head, he saw the shadows on her smooth features.

'You're just tired,' he said. 'You get some sleep, you'll feel better, and then we can go on. You'll see.'

She turned and stared at him. 'Don't you get it, Larry? That boy is dead. And the other one, they say he's just gonna be a vegetable. His brain was damaged too bad, and there ain't anything they can do.'

Yes, yes, he thought. Some good old southern boys got themselves in the wrong place at the wrong time, and somebody squashed them, but what does that have to do with anything? Nothing to do with Mister Larry Rosenweig, that was for sure. Why couldn't he get Mellie to see this? Sometimes, though he knew he was speaking in English, it seemed he was talking in a foreign tongue, and that what he thought was perfectly clear as he spoke it came out like Urdu or Sanskrit to these people. It made him want to tear his hair sometimes.

'Mellie, it was an accident, that's all. It doesn't

change things. What we are doing is right, why can't you see that?'

But she stared right back at him. 'Is it, Larry? This whole town's split right down the middle, and half the kids aren't talking to their parents at all any more. And now this. Lucas says it was probably the Kluckers, but—'

'*Lucas!*' He spat out the name, hating it. Ever since Mellie had called him at the boarding house and told him she wanted to talk, for some reason he'd been thinking about Lucas Buck. He had shaken Lucas's hand, but the next day, away from the strange, syrupy aura that man seemed to project, he'd wondered why he'd done it.

Hadn't Lucas Buck been the real reason he'd come back to this disgusting town in the first place? Not for this protest shit, although that was how it had turned out, but to redeem himself, to slay the malignant dragons of memory. To heal the ulcer of his humiliation at the hands of Lucas Buck. Lucas!

And then, finally, he saw it.

'Lucas Buck said it was the Klan?'

She moved her shoulders. 'He didn't say for sure, but he said it looked like their work.'

'Uh huh. Funny thing. You know he warned me of the same thing, said to watch out for the Kluckers, the night before it happened?'

'He told you that?'

'Damned straight he did. Do you see any

coincidence to that, Mellie? Do you believe in co-incidence?'

He put his hand on her shoulder, but she pulled away. 'I don't see what you're trying to say, Larry. You don't think Lucas killed that poor boy, do you?'

His hand hovered in the air a moment, before he suddenly noticed it was still suspended there, and dropped it to his lap. The two lines over the bridge of his nose wrinkled sharply as he concentrated, trying to work it out. He could almost see the connection, and he was sure if he looked just a little harder, he could—

Ah.

'No, Mellie, he didn't do it. He's too much of a coward for that. But here you go, he comes to me and warns me about the Klan. And before you can even turn around, two innocent kids get jumped, and the next day after that, Lucas Buck is telling *you* the Klan did it. Don't you see? Somehow he set it up. And now you're going to go along with him, swallow his little scheme, and leave me high and dry. Mellie, can't you *see*?'

But she had leaned back away from his ve-hemence, because what she did see was what had bothered her about Larry Rosenweig all along: the way his eyes got to shining and bulging, and how his voice would begin to sound almost as if some-body had put their hands around his neck and begun to squeeze him tight; the ugly flush that would colour his cheeks as he spoke so quickly the words backed up in his throat. In a word, Larry Rosenweig looked *crazy*, and Mellie was beginning to think she was jinxed.

Crazy men; the only people she ever seemed to get hooked up with were all crazy. First Gage, and now this boy whom she hardly knew, sitting there breathing stale pizza and obsession into her face like some kind of unhinged human furnace. She recoiled in disgust.

'Larry, you're talking nothin' but craziness. Why would Lucas do anything like that? How could he? It don't make any sense.'

But Larry missed completely all her warning signs and burned on, intent on self-immolation.

'Mellie, it's plain as anything. He's after you. He's been after you since that day out on the highway. He didn't have to treat me the way he did, he only did it to make him look bigger in your eyes. Come on, Mellie. Come *on*.'

For a moment, almost caught in his heated phantasmic web, she considered it. Lucas? Wanting her? But that didn't make any sense, either. Oh, Christine might have mused on it – what had she said? That he was quality? Well, sure, but that made it all the more ridiculous. The likes of Mellie Hankings didn't hook up to people like Lucas Buck, no matter what kind of catch her older sister might have made. No, Gage Temple, if the awful truth were told, was more like it.

And speaking of which, surely that was nothing out at the river, the night Lucas had stopped Gage in the middle of raping her. What had he said? She'd heard it as she limped away, him muttering something over Gage's unconscious body. Something about a deal. And then there was Gage's raving about Lucas wanting her for himself ... but that couldn't mean anything. Could it?

Of course not. But for a moment she wavered, until Larry went ahead and nailed himself right up to the barn door.

'Mellie, don't you get it?' he whispered intently, his eyes now glassy and dazed. 'Lucas is a murderer, whether he did the actual killing or not. He's responsible, and he did it to get at you. So if you go along with it, that makes you no better than he is. It makes you a murderer too.'

He said the last word in a low, hollow croak that was so ridiculous and melodramatic it made her want to slap him. What kind of madness did he think he was saying?

'Larry, that's it. That's enough. You're nothing but a ... a paranormal, or whatever.'

He heard it in her voice, and knew he'd lost once again. Old Larry Rosenweig wasn't any Mister for her, he was just plain old Jew-boy Larry, and his money wasn't any good at all. Not with her, not any more.

And the hell with it, then. It wasn't really her fault, poor little ignorant redneck girl. He knew who to blame. And he knew what to do. For one moment in the midst of his mania, he remembered what Lucas had said, Lucas's *deal*: 'All you need to do is remember that I'm your friend.'

Well, that was one deal he had *no* intention of keeping; (although he felt an odd, worrisome twinge as he came to that conclusion – and there had been another deal, too, hadn't there?). His thin lips widened in a bitter, knowing smile. 'That's paranoid, Mellie. Not paranormal, the word is paranoid.' He shrugged. 'Not that it matters any more. I guess your mind is made up?'

The sneer stuck like a burr just beneath the saddle of her skin. She stood up. 'You're an asshole, Larry. That's what your problem is. You don't care about those two poor boys, all you care about is you. This protest don't mean nothing to you, and I don't either. Ain't that about right, Larry?'

He squinted up at her. The sun blazed from behind her head like a corona. Why, yes, she had him, she was exactly right, and so the fuck what? At least *her* money was good in Trinity, although she would never understand precisely what that meant to him.

He pictured himself playing this scene in a movie, and wondered what his next lines were supposed to be. What would Mister Rosenweig say now?

'It's all right, Mellie. I understand. Go on and

live your own life . . . it's yours, and you can't help it.'

Yes, he thought. Exactly right.

But she only stared at him, then said, 'God, what an asshole you are.' Then she turned and walked away, and all he could think was: LUCAS BUCK LUCAS BUCK LUCAS BUCK.

Ben Healy was standing in front of the Rice Jewelers, admiring one of the sample rings for the Trinity High School senior class, and thinking about how fine one of them would look on his own hand, when somebody slapped him hard on the shoulder.

'Huh – say *what*?'

'Here,' Larry Rosenweig said, thrusting a folded sheet of paper at him. 'Give this to your fucking good buddy, Lucas.'

And he was gone.

Ben shook his head. Now what the fuck was *that* all about? He looked down at the paper. There was nothing on the outside, just a sheet of paper that looked as if it had been torn out of a school notebook you could buy at any drugstore.

It was a note for Lucas. But it wasn't taped shut or anything, and he couldn't imagine what that Yankee boy, all steamed up like he'd been, would want to say to Lucas.

He shrugged, glanced around, then opened it

up. It took him a moment to get the drift of Larry's hasty scrawl, but he finally got it deciphered:

I know those two kids were your doing. Meet me out on the highway beyond the river bridge tonight at midnight. We'll settle this once and for all.

It was signed only with the letter 'L'.

Ben stared. Now what the hell could this be about? Finally he shook his head, shrugged, refolded the note and put it in his shirt pocket. He glanced at the gold wedding clock on the top shelf in Rice's window. One-thirty. Lucas would probably still be at home, this time of day.

Marvis Pickney stepped out of the revolving door of the Piggly Wiggly and headed for his truck in the parking lot.

'Hey, Marvis, wait up.'

He turned. 'Well, hey, Lucas.' Marvis felt a momentary flash of discomfort. He knew that if Gage saw him talking to Lucas, he'd give him pure hell for his disloyalty, but as for himself, he figured Lucas hadn't actually done anything to him. So he held up and waited.

'Listen, Marvis, I got something for you to give to Gage, if you see him. You goin' out there this afternoon?'

Marvis nodded.

'That's fine, then,' Lucas said. 'Listen, it's important, you just give him this note, here.' Lucas handed over a folded piece of notepaper. 'You do that OK?'

'Sure, Lucas. No problem. Uh, is things better between you and Gage?'

But Lucas only stared at him blankly. 'Why, Marvis? Is something supposed to be wrong between me and him?'

It was too much for Marvis. Ambiguity was something far beyond his minimal coping abilities. He just shrugged. Lucas looked at him quizzically, his head cocked, then grinned, turned, and walked away.

Of course Marvis opened the note, but it didn't mean anything to him. He couldn't read a lick at all. But he did understand how it was signed. He'd managed to pick up the letters of the alphabet, more or less. And there she was, the letter 'L', plain as day.

L for Lucas, he figured, pleased with himself.

Chapter Eleven

The handsome Georgian brick building just off Oleander Drive on Willow Street, in the heart of downtown Trinity, had been the home of the Merchant's National Bank for almost a hundred years. Five generations of farmers and shop-keepers had gone through its tall doorway, flanked by generous white pillars, twisting their caps and hats in their hands, to ask for loans. In most cases they had got them, for the 'Merchants', as it was simply known, had never gone in for the fancy kind of big city banking. Management had invested in land and buildings and home mort-gages from the very beginning, a policy that had served them well. During the great panic of the Depression years, the Merchants had felt hardly a quiver.

The current president of the bank, Orville Willis, was always pleased to welcome large depositors, as he was dutifully doing now, to his spacious, bay-windowed and oak-panelled office with its view overlooking the front door.

'Coffee, Christopher?' he asked. The thing everybody noticed about Orville was his thinness. Thin body, thin hair, thin lips. A thin smile. He smiled that way now, and inclined his head while he waited for Preacher Buck's reply.

The Preacher, wearing a rumpled dark green suit from Robert Hall with a wide, flowered tie, settled back in the soft leather club chair in front of Orville's mahogany desk. 'That would be nice, Orville. Two sugars, lots of cream.'

Willis flipped a switch on his old-fashioned wooden intercom box. 'Susie? Two coffees, please. Sugar and cream for the Reverend, and make mine black.'

They made small talk about the weather – good for the crops – and the sad condition of kids these days. Hippies and Communists, most of them, at least in the wide world beyond Trinity. And right here in town, that poor murdered negro boy. And Ted Hendricks's son, too – likely to be a turnip for as long as he lived. Just plain awful, it was.

But as the small talk faded, Preacher Buck felt an unaccustomed nervousness; it wasn't often he came to anybody hat in hand – although that wasn't precisely the case here. Orville, like most men in town with any power or authority, owed him more than a few favours.

Susie, who was sixtyish, white-haired, dumpy, and didn't look like a Susie at all, brought in the coffee on a fine silver tray, which she placed on the front of Orville's desk so both men could reach their cups easily. Preacher Buck took his, sipped, and nodded approval. 'Good.'

After Orville had bestowed one parsimonious smile of approval on his own portion, he patted his lips with a clean hanky and said, 'Well, then, Christopher, to what do I owe the pleasure?'

The Reverend cleared his throat, still not quite used to this strange feeling of supplication that seemed to have seized him. And it was ridiculous, of course. Why should he feel that way with Orville Willis? By any standards of sanity, Orville should be more than happy to jump to his tune. He'd made Orville a lot of money over the years, and if he would go along on this, he would soon make him a lot more. Nevertheless, Preacher Buck couldn't shake his unease, and so to cover it, he forced himself into a briskness he didn't feel.

'Well, here's the deal, Orville. The widow Hendricks wants to sell out, and I aim to do the buying.'

At that, Orville's customary bland expression smartened up immediately. He pursed his thin lips and uttered a soft whistle. 'She does? And she wants to sell to you?'

The Preacher shifted. He didn't entirely understand this part himself. But he hadn't got to where he was by doing a lot of dental examinations on gift horses.

'She's asked me to make her an offer, yes.'

'Ah . . .' Orville said, after a moment's thought. 'I see.'

'Do you?'

The banker steepled his long, slender fingers beneath his narrow chin. 'It's a big mouthful to bite off, Christopher. You got the teeth for it?'

'Well, that's the problem. The way she wants the deal structured, it's gonna take a lot of upfront cash. More than I got, to tell the truth. I'm a little cash poor at the moment.'

Willis chuckled softly. 'Oh, come now, Christopher. I can't believe a man like you wouldn't have a fruit jar or two buried out in the back yard.'

The Preacher nodded firmly. 'Who doesn't, these days? But that's unmarked money, Orville. The IRS don't know a thing about it. Now, I can dig it up – let's say there is, for the sake of argument, maybe two hundred grand in these fruit jars – but if I do, I'm still short. So what you could do is let me squeeze all those wrinkled hundred dollar bills through you, along with another hundred grand in sweetening from your side. Say a short-term loan of three hundred, all told?'

Orville Willis leaned back in his chair, which let out a minor shriek of protest. What the Preacher was proposing was entirely illegal, and if discovered by the proper parties – say, anybody working for a government agency that spelled its name with initials – there would be long jail terms all around. But that wasn't what worried him. What the government didn't know wouldn't hurt it, and there was a lot that went on in small town financial circles the government would never find out about.

'Christopher, I imagine we could work something out along those lines. But won't that leave you with a bad case of the shorts? I'm going to take a hefty bite of interest out of your hide, you know.'

The Preacher felt some of his worry lift. This was the kind of talk he could deal with. He grinned widely. 'Well, of course you will, Orville. And so you should. But the cash is only tied up in escrow for ninety days. After that, I take her paper and we fix up all the loose ends. Some of which, I imagine, will be pretty loose.'

They understood each other perfectly. After another fifteen minutes of conversation, they shook on it. Not much would be on paper, not of the real deal. But it would happen. Orville stood up and leaned forward over his desk.

'Going to clean you out for a while, Christopher. You won't have a pot to piss in for those ninety days.'

Preacher Buck shrugged. 'I ain't got that many day-to-day expenses, Orville. I'll make out fine, don't you worry.'

'Well, that's good then.'

They shook hands again, and that was that.

*   *   *

'Who give you this?' Gage Temple said, not noticing that his thick fingers had begun to quiver uncontrollably.

Marvis Pickney stared at him and wondered what the hell he'd gone and done now. Gage didn't look happy at all. In fact, with his face suddenly turned the colour of spoiled cottage cheese, Gage looked downright sick. Not for the first time, Marvis wished he'd stayed in school long enough to learn how to read. That note he'd just handed over must have been a real pisser.

'I told you, Gage. It was Lucas Buck. He handed it to me right in front of the Rice Jewelry.' Marvis wasn't what anybody would call quick, but even he noticed Gage wince at the mention of yet another sore spot on his much-thumped hide, though Marvis didn't understand about the wedding ring Gage had thrown in the river, and which he was still committed to paying old man Rice for.

Gage read the note again. It was no better the second time through. A black rage of confusion began to boil in his skull. Lucas Buck! Would he never get shot of that bastard?

He glared at Marvis. 'Well, is that it? You got anything else for me today?'

Marvis was totally confused now. He looked down, shuffled his feet, then shifted his gaze to

some vague spot beyond Gage's broad shoulders.
'Well, Gage, actually there was. One little thing.'

'So? Go on, boy, spit it out, and then take yourself off. I got some thinking to do.'

'Wait a minute, then.'

Marvis went over to his pickup, fished around in the back for a second, and came up with a lumpy burlap sack. He hauled it out and dragged it over to Gage. Whatever was inside made a thick, wooden thumping sound. He dropped the bag at Gage's feet, stuck his hands inside the front pockets of his jeans, and shrugged.

'What's that, Marvis?'

'It's a burlap sack, Gage.'

'I can see that, you idjit. What's *in* it?'

Marvis shrugged. 'I dunno, Gage. Cousin Earl told me not to open her up.'

Gage stared at him. 'Cousin Earl gave it to you?'

'Uh huh. He told me to get rid of it where nobody would find her. But Gage, you know I ain't the smartest thing. I thought and thought, and I couldn't figger out a place where nobody could trip across it. So I thought maybe you could help me out?'

Something lifted faint wings in the back of Gage's swirling thoughts. Cousin Earl? Now what would Cousin Earl be so hot to get rid of?

'All right, Marvis. You leave her here and don't worry about it no more. I'll take care of it.'

Marvis grinned suddenly, like a kid who's just

had a huge problem lifted off his shoulders. 'Well, that's fine of you, Gage. I do appreciate it.'

'Go on, Marvis, get on home. I got some things to take care of, OK?'

Marvis nodded. 'I'll be seein' you then, Gage.'

'Uh huh.' But Gage had already lifted the bag and turned away, and he paid no more attention to Marvis Pickney. He took the bag up onto his porch, set it down, and pulled a scarred pocket knife out of his jeans. There were three or four twists of brown twine around the neck of the bag. He sliced through, shook the bag open, and reached in.

He pulled out a sawed-off baseball bat with black tape wrapped around the handle. The thick, heavy head of the bat had black crusts on it, and dark, runny stains. He raised the bat, sniffed at it, and wrinkled his nose.

Then he sat down on the top step, put his elbows on his knees and his chin on his fists, and did some hard, heavy thinking.

So Lucas knew about how Gage had set loose the Pickney clan, did he? And he wanted to settle things once and for all? Gage took out the note, smoothed it, and read it again. He looked over at the bag, and at the grisly relic sitting on top of the burlap. The tape was good. Gage watched his cop shows, and he knew about fingerprints. But the tape wouldn't take fingerprints. That might be a problem. Still, maybe the science boys could tell whose blood and brains had dried on that old bat.

Probably they could. If so, the fact that the whole Pickney clan was stupid as posts just might finally work out for something useful.

So Lucas wants to settle once and for all? Well, so do I, Gage thought grimly.

Gage pulled over in the middle of the river bridge and stopped. He got out, went around the back of his pickup, and hauled out the burlap bag. He dropped the bag, then walked to the end of the bridge and hunted around till he found some rocks of a size he thought would do. He carried them back, stuffed them in the bag, and re-tied the top. Then he took a final look around.

The fog was in heavy tonight. It curled around the girders of the bridge and crept like whipped cream along the surface of the water below. The air felt thick enough to chew. He cocked an ear; he knew that sound carried in funny ways when the weather was like this. But he couldn't hear anything but the damp rush of the river. He tossed the bag over and listened to the splash. No reason anybody would look, and the rocks should be enough to weight down the bag. He climbed back into his truck, drove off the bridge and kept on going till he pulled off again, about a half mile on down the road. He parked well back. Nobody driving by would see the truck unless they knew to look for it. He locked it up, took a deep breath, squared his shoulders, and started walking quietly back towards the bridge.

The sawed-off bat was a comforting weight in his hand.

Larry Rosenweig had smoked a bowl of pot before he started out, but after the long walk, it had pretty well worn off, and he was feeling the chill of the mist and his own fear.

Mister Rosenweig? Well, hell, yes, but he doubted that Lucas Buck would give much of a shit for that. Nevertheless, he intended to have it out with that redneck SOB. For a little while there, he had almost come around – but then Lucas had shown his true colours.

He wondered about Mellie. It was obvious what Lucas was trying to do. And almost, he could admire the sheer snakiness of it. Lucas was working for his daddy, no doubt about it, and he'd done a pretty fair job. Larry had tried to call a few of the people who'd been with him, but they were all too scared even to talk to him now. The beating and murder had done that, and though Larry wasn't completely sure just how Lucas had handled that, he knew he was behind it somehow. Just as he was behind Mellie changing her mind.

He wrapped his arms around his chest for a little warmth and stamped his feet. The clearing off the side of the road was small and full of shadows and surrounded by walls of thick brush. Overhead the moon was little more than a Cheshire smile, casting almost no light. Spooky place, and anybody could be hiding in those bushes. But Larry didn't think that was Lucas's style. No, Lucas would come driving up in that GTO, big as life and twice as arrogant, and then—

Well, then, what?

Larry looked up at the sky. Well, then, he – Mister Larry Rosenweig – was just going to kick his ass till he screamed. No switchblades tonight, just man to man. He knew he could take Lucas in a fair fight. Lucas was a bully and a coward, after all. You could tell that just from his slimy deals. And a brave man could always take a coward, especially if he knew he was right.

Larry tried to spit, but his mouth was dry. The pot, no doubt. Imagine thinking he could make deals. Larry had remembered the first deal – that Larry gave Mellie to Lucas. And what kind of shit was that? You couldn't just give another person to somebody like a loaf of bread.

He felt his thoughts beginning to ratchet. Somehow things were getting more and more confused. He wished he had a little pot left, to calm himself down.

He heard an engine coming up, and stepped back into the brush until the sound passed on by. It didn't sound like a high-powered GTO engine, but Larry was no expert. He stayed back until the sound vanished on down the road. Then he stepped out again and stood there, waiting.

Gage came from around the back, through the undergrowth. He had no intention of just walking up to Lucas. Not for what he had in mind. But Gage was a country boy, and slipping through the brush, even with mist hanging off everything like soggy cotton, was no problem for him.

He heard somebody cough up ahead, and quickened his pace. His heart was pounding, and his forehead felt like it was on fire. The pain in his taped ribs was enough to clamp his teeth like a vice, but he kept on going.

Lucas was going to get a lot more than a few cracked ribs. Oh, yes, indeed.

Larry heard it before he saw anything. In fact, he never did really *see* the big, shadowy shape that seemed to lunge out of the darkness. He half-turned, and just managed to get one hand up, before a great, clubbing blow broke most of the bones in his right arm.

The pain was like a railroad spike driven through his elbow, but it only lasted an instant. The next blow crashed into his skull and he fell, a single scream choked and dying in his throat.

* * *

Gage stood over the fallen figure, panting, the bat raised to strike again. 'Got you, Lucas,' he gasped.

He looked down. Lucas jerked on the ground at his feet. He made a short, snoring sound, then moaned. Gage knew what he had to do, but he wanted Lucas to see it coming. He bent over and rolled him onto his back. And stopped, his face frozen in shock.

It wasn't Lucas. It was that Yankee boy.

'Please . . .' Larry Rosenweig said.

Gage dropped the bat and ran.

Lucas was almost back up to the river bridge, dragging his soggy burden along, when he saw Gage's pickup roar past, swerving and fishtailing, as if all the demons in hell were in hot pursuit. He grinned and continued on. Busy, busy. So much to do. Idle hands and the devil's work and all.

He popped open the trunk of the GTO and dumped the bag inside. Then he slammed down the lid and ambled on up the road. It only took a couple of minutes to find the clear patch off the side of the road, and a minute beyond that to find Larry.

'That you, Mister Rosenweig?' he said, squatting down.

To Larry, it seemed that his nemesis had

appeared as some nightmarish apparition. He'd seen the one who had clubbed him, and it wasn't Lucas. But here was Lucas now. Maybe he'd been wrong?

It was so hard to think. The world would go all reddish grey, and slabs of pain would radiate from his arm and his skull. Then things would pop back in for a second, and then begin to fade again.

He knew he was badly hurt. And he was cold, so cold, and he'd never been so scared in his life.

'Lucas . . .'

Lucas nodded cheerfully. 'Told you, boy. Made you a real nice deal. Two of them, in fact. All you had to do was think of me as a friend, Larry. That was all. But you couldn't do that, could you?'

He reached down to his waist and caressed his belt buckle absently. 'Larry, did you really think I'd let you get away with it? Did you think you could do that to *me*?'

Larry felt his face go numb. He realized he couldn't feel anything in his legs. 'Help me . . .'

'Sure thing, Larry. Here you go. Oopsy daisy, wait just a minute, OK?'

Lucas stood up, put his hands in his back pockets, and wandered off. 'When nature calls, Larry. Just be a sec. You hang on, there.'

But of course Larry couldn't hang on. The bubble of blood growing beneath his crushed skull was spreading now, stretching, pressing down on the torn and bruised tissue beneath. Larry blinked, but somebody had turned out the lights, and all he could see was the blood-tinged dark. Now he couldn't feel the pain in his arm anymore, and that was a blessing, but he understood it was not a good sign.

Nothing was a good sign, not anymore.

The cold crept up, then, and clamped icy fingers on his chest. He thought about Milton, and wondered what his mother would say, to the shame of him dying like this beside a nameless southern road.

'Oh, Daddy,' he whispered, and then, to his sudden joy, Milton was there, smiling, lifting him up, carrying him away, and he never noticed the sudden burst of red, spreading deep inside his ruined brain.

Lucas finished his business and zipped up. 'You know, you shake and shake, and damn if that last drop don't go down your drawers anyway.' He ambled slowly back to where Larry had begun to make long, wet, snoring noises.

After a moment Larry began to quiver, then to buck like a beached catfish. His movements quickly crescendoed, and then, finally, his frenzied heaves slowly lessened until, at the end, there was only the faint drumming of his heels in the dirt.

When Lucas was sure the show was over, he stretched, then squatted down again. He unbuckled his belt and took it off. What little light there was winked softly off the big silver buckle. It was easy to pick out the name Gage, worked in gold on the silver backing. He ran the belt through the buckle to make a loop, which he placed, with tender care, around Larry Rosenweig's neck.

'Now, don't you worry, Mister Rosenweig. This one's on me. See, your money's no good around here. No good at all.' He yanked the loop tight. He paused, but there was no reaction from Larry, and so he dusted off his hands and stood up again. His knees made a soft, popping noise. Lucas sighed.

'See, Larry, the thing is, you should have never kicked that dent in my car door.'

He turned and left the clearing, whistling softly. The tune was one of his favourites: the Beatles song, 'Money Can't Buy You Love'.

Thanks to an anonymous call, the police discovered Larry Rosenweig's body less than half an hour later.

Better late than never, Lucas thought.

Gage Temple ran straight home. He slewed the pickup into his dusty front yard, slammed to a halt, and staggered out. As soon as his feet hit the ground the cramps seized him. He belched, a great gassy eruption, then bent over and puked until dry heaves tied him in a knot.

After a while, arms wrapped around his belly, his breath coming in huge, whooping gulps, he shambled up his porch steps. There his legs gave out completely, and he sank to the floor.

His mind was a ball of black fire, whirling. He couldn't get his grip on anything at all. What the hell had that Yankee boy been doing there?

Frantically, he tried to piece it together. Had he killed that boy? He didn't know. The kid had been alive, but for how long? Then the terrible gravity of what he had done hit him, and he found himself praying fervently that Larry didn't stay alive. That boy had seen his face!

With icy clarity, he tried to recall that terrible blow. He could still feel the awful weight of it, and the mushy sensation as he drove the bat home. Like hitting a ripe melon with a hammer. There had been a finality to it, and he doubted that, if Larry didn't get help right away, he would make it.

All right, all right. *Think*! If the boy died, was he in the clear? Grimly, he tried to force the pictures to come. He'd dropped the bat, but that didn't make any difference, did it? They couldn't get fingerprints. And nobody had seen him, had they?

So. Was there any connection between him and Larry? Marvis had given him the note, but Marvis couldn't read. So he wouldn't know anything, and even if he did, he would assume it was Lucas that Gage had been going to meet.

Slowly, his racing heart began to wind down. He

shook his head. His ribs ached like fire – he'd put his weight behind that baseball bat. OK. So what would the cops find?

He thought about that, and as he pieced it together, a light began to gleam in the chaos of his terror. What they would find was another hippy, beaten to death with a bat that had the brains of earlier victims on it. And nothing to connect it to Gage, except—

No, Marvis had never opened the bag. He might guess what was inside, but he couldn't know for sure. It was all what the cop shows would call circumstantial evidence, and now that he could see it clearly, pretty thin evidence, at that.

He whooshed out a long sigh. Maybe, just maybe, he would ride this thing out OK. But what had happened to Lucas? How did he fit in?

Gage couldn't even begin to get his head around that one, but maybe it didn't matter. Not for a while, at least.

He glanced up at the sky. The stars were coming clear again, and it looked as if the fog was lifting. Only a few stray trails of mist snaked along his yard. Suddenly he was freezing. His teeth began to chatter, and his bones felt as if they were shivering out of his skin.

Well, he knew what to do about that. And it wouldn't be a bad medicine for the rest of what ailed him at the moment. The cardboard carton with four jars of shine was still where he'd left it, just to the right of the top of the steps. Within easy reach.

Gage reached. He poured down the first jar as if it were nothing more than pure spring water. The night had cooled down the shine, and it chilled his burning throat as it warmed his shrivelled, empty belly.

After he finished the first jar, he felt so much better that he drank two more. When the police arrived, three hours after that, he was as dead to the world as the stones in his barren front yard.

He wouldn't come out of it till twelve hours later, just as deputy Collier Jackson was opening the door to let Lucas Buck into his dirty, stinking cell.

Chapter Twelve

'Terrible thing,' Heppy Hankings remarked, as Mellie poured some two per cent on her morning bowl of Cheerios. Josh grunted from behind his *Guardian* and rattled the sheets in agreement. Josh wasn't much for breakfast table conversation, but he did toss out one grumbling nugget. 'Damned Commie. Served him right.'

Heppy didn't add to that, but her eyes darted towards her daughter, as if expecting some reply. Mellie raised her eyes from her cereal. 'What? What are you two talking about?'

Josh only snapped his paper again, but Heppy said, 'Heard it on the radio this morning. That Yankee fellow that was agitating against the Preacher's war memorial, he went and got himself killed.'

To Mellie, this news, delivered so calmly in the room where she'd taken breakfast all her life, a room filled with familiar smells, a room awash in the soft morning summer light, had the same effect as if her mother had reached across the table and punched her in the nose. Her mouth fell open.

'I don't . . . what? Larry? Dead?'

Heppy eyed her sharply. 'You knew that boy, didn't you?'

And Josh, positively loquacious for that time of day, added from behind his paper, 'If I was you, little girl, and I did know that Yankee bastard, I'd keep my blowhole shut about it.'

Automatically she spooned up another bite of Cheerios and tried to chew, but it was like trying to get down a mouthful of library paste. She stopped, and for one wild moment, considered spitting out the whole gluey wad onto the red-checked plastic tablecloth.

Instead, she swallowed. 'What . . . happened?'

Heppy seemed to take a grim satisfaction in recounting the story. 'Found him out by the river bridge, his head stove in like a rotten egg. Dead as a doornail, and with Gage Temple's belt strapped up around his neck like a hangman's noose.'

'You got that Hankings luck with men, daughter,' Josh growled. 'First Gage, and now that hippy boy. Commies and murderers.'

'Oh, Daddy.' She felt the tears begin to burn, and suddenly wanted to be any place but here, sitting in this worn, familiar room, with Heppy's stern, judgemental gaze boring a hole in her.

Outside, in the street, a car honked, two long, loud blasts.

'Now what in tarnation . . . ?' Josh grumbled,

lowering his paper. 'Huh. Third bad one of three. It's that Buck boy, ain't it, Mellie? He one of yours too?'

Mellie craned her neck to see. Lucas was parked at the curb, the top down on the bright red GTO. He waved.

'I'm goin',' Mellie said abruptly. She ripped the napkin out of the neck of her T-shirt and slapped it down on the table.

'Now, Mellie, you just wait a minute,' Heppy said, sudden concern in her tone. But she was too late.

The screen door slammed, and she was talking to the empty air.

'Damned kids,' Josh observed.

'Oh, shut up, you old fool.'

'Watch your mouth, woman, or I'll put my hand to you.'

So they continued, their hellish rut warm and familiar, and left the strange events of the day forgotten. It was, after all, Trinity, and corpses did have a way of turning up, every now and then.

'Climb in there, Mellie.'

'Oh, Lucas, have you heard?'

He glanced over at her, his expression bland. 'You mean about Larry and Gage? Shame, isn't it?'

'What have you heard, Lucas? What happened?

It's crazy! First that poor negro boy and his friend, and now Larry.'

Lucas slipped the car into gear and pulled away from the curb, the big engine bubbling softly through the twin glasspaks. 'It's a good thing, then, I guess,' he said.

'What are you talking about? Ain't nothing good about any of this.' Mellie felt as if she were trying to slug her way out of a mental pillow fight. For the last several days – hell, weeks – every man she'd tried to talk sense to might as well have been on Mars. It really was like they spoke different languages. She'd say one thing, they'd reply with something else, something totally off the wall.

It was crazy. Maybe she'd heard wrong.

'What'd you say?'

Lucas flicked the turn signal, slowed, then turned left on Oleander and headed for the centre of town. 'I said it was a good thing. Funny how stuff always seems to turn out right.'

She shook her head. Nope. This was just as crazy as the first thing he'd said. Two boys dead, and her would-be fiancé charged with killing one of them? And there was something awfully wrong to the feel of that idea, too, wasn't there?

'Lucas, have you lost your mind?' A tiny nubbin of thought picked at her attention, then got it. 'What have you heard about Gage?' she asked again.

He shrugged. 'What does it matter, Mellie? I told

you that you'd never have to worry about him again. That was our deal, remember? One of them, at least. And look at what happened. That's what I mean about everything turning out just fine.'

She felt her mouth fall slightly open. 'Lucas, I got no idea what you think you're talking about, but that is just plain crazy. It's terrible what Gage done. If he done it. Are they sure about that?'

Abruptly Lucas downshifted and swerved to the right. Seemingly by accident he ended up in one of the slanted parking spots along the edge of the town square. He turned off the engine and swivelled in his seat until he faced her head on.

'Now, why would you think any different, Mellie? There wasn't any love lost between Larry and Gage, was there? I got better reason than most to know how Gage feels about you, right? And maybe he noticed you and Larry sniffing each other up, just like I did. Only Gage took it into his head to do something about it.'

'Wait a minute. You ain't saying that Gage – that because of *me*—' She shook her head wildly. 'That don't make sense, Lucas. It just don't, not at all.'

But he only grinned at her. 'Mellie, you think too much good of people. Old Gage, he flat out raped you. If I hadn't come along when I did, how do you know they wouldn't have found you floating face down in the river the next morning?'

And that stopped her, because in more than one dreadful dream after that night, it had turned out

226

exactly that way, and she would wake in her bed, feeling the cold rush of river water filling her lungs.

'Old Gage, he's got a temper on him,' Lucas added. 'You know that's the truth, Mellie. So why have you got such a problem with all this?'

But something inside her still resisted, even though, for some reason, Lucas suddenly seemed the most reasonable man in the world. He radiated an air of calm and absolute plausibility. So why couldn't she believe him?

'Well . . . how do they know it was Gage? Did they catch him? Did he confess or something?'

Lucas shook his head. A bunch of young kids, one waving a lime-green hula hoop, rushed past, heading for the open space at the centre of the square. A pair of old fogeys seated on one of the white benches started yelling at each other. One wadded up his newspaper and threw it on the ground. The other one waved his cane threateningly.

Lucas reached up and tweezed his lower lip between his thumb and index finger thoughtfully. Finally he said, 'No, they didn't catch him, not in the act. And a friend of mine at the jail says he was out like a light when they picked him up. They did a blood alcohol on him to see if they needed to take him to the hospital. He was so out of it they were worried, and then he turned up three times legal drunk. Enough to kill a normal human, but for

Gage, just another bender. He's still sleeping it off. They figure he'll be up and about by this afternoon.'

'Well, if he was that drunk—'

'Mellie, there was more. Larry's head was bashed in with a baseball bat, and the county mounties think it might be one of the weapons used on the Hendricks boy and his black buddy. And then, of course, there was the clincher.'

It was slowly sinking in, although the idea of it was so alien, so awful, she still really couldn't get around all of it. Gage involved with the other killing, too?

'What was the clincher?' she whispered.

'Gage's belt, that big old fancy silver one with his name in gold. They found it wrapped around Larry's neck, tight as a rabbit's dirty back road.'

Why, yes, hadn't her daddy Josh said something about that? But that couldn't be, could it—

And with that, she knew.

She looked into Lucas's eyes and saw that he knew she knew. And he didn't care.

She remembered it as clearly as any other awful thing that imprinted itself on your mind and would never fade. Trudging up the path from the river she had paused, like Lot's wife, and turned back – to see Lucas pick up that distinctive belt of Gage's, its silver buckle winking in the moonlight, and fold it up.

'You . . .' she said softly. 'It was you . . .'

Preacher Buck checked the numbers in his personal chequing account one more time, then flipped the chequebook shut and tossed it across his cluttered desk top, where it landed on the folded up copy of the morning's *Guardian*.

He sighed. Strange days, it seemed. Now what the hell did Gage Temple think he was doing? He closed his eyes and tried to unravel that particular ball of twine, but couldn't quite grasp the end he needed to pull. Would it have any effect on his plans for the memorial?

He finally decided that it wouldn't. If anything, it helped things along. And that made sense, didn't it? All his life he'd been accustomed to things just happening, and happening in such a way that whatever plans he had got helped along. Funny about Gage, though. He wouldn't have thought it of that old boy.

He glanced out his window. The afternoon sun slanted in. Off to the right, he could see a pool of shadow, out beyond his orchard. Yes, things just happened, and wasn't it a blessing? He wondered if Lucas, who had chosen to oppose him, was noticing. If his son had intended to win this argument, he must now be starting to understand just how little chance of that still existed.

The Preacher could sniff the prevailing winds as well as anybody, and his sniffer was telling him it was all over but the shouting. Any organized opposition to the memorial would collapse now, with that Yankee's murder, and the rest of it. A shame, really, but that wasn't the Preacher's problem.

His hand crept towards the black telephone on his desk. Should he give Lucas a call? Maybe invite him over, let him surrender in private? He might take it easier if his pride was intact. The lesson, it seemed to the Preacher, was just about complete. Lucas couldn't renounce – and how he hated that word – his own blood, the legacy of his family, and hope to compete with his father afterwards. There would come a time, once Lucas was safely back in the fold, when the power would be his to wield. Not right away, of course, but sometime down the road. When the Preacher was ready to lay it down.

Or, more likely, when Lucas was strong enough to take it.

He rubbed the side of his nose, considering. Now that it was almost over, he had to admit that, once or twice, he'd had his doubts. Had his time come? Could Lucas have beaten him, taken the power from him for his own?

But now it seemed that he couldn't. Go his own way? Renounce?

Bullshit to that. And so we go, he reflected, to more important matters. He glanced at his cheque-book and chuckled softly. He was, and would be for the next three months or so, effectively as poor as a churchmouse. As poor as a country preacher. The thought amused him, without lessening the truth of it.

He'd gone out in the dead of night with a garden spade, down to the end of the orchard, and dug under a gnarled apple tree. Twenty sealed glass fruit jars had come up, etched cloudy from the acid in the bitter earth, but what was inside was OK. Which was good, because each jar contained two tight rolls of hundred dollar bills – a hundred of them to a roll, twenty thousand cash money to a jar. Orville Willis hadn't found anything wrong with the money when he'd dumped it out of a battered briefcase onto his desk, either.

Now everything was tied up in escrow, awaiting the close of the deal with Georgina Hendricks. And even that was a testimony, wasn't it? He'd had his eyes on Georgina's holding ever since her husband had passed on, but he'd figured he'd have to wait a while. Something had changed the old biddy's mind, though, speeded her up a little. Just another one of those things that happened. Happened so fortuitously, for him. It was almost as if his power, or his luck, was working overtime to prove to Lucas how ineffectual he was without that power. It might be in the Buck blood, but it must be acknowledged. It couldn't be *renounced*, he thought with satisfaction. It just didn't work that way. The only way to have it was to *serve* it.

Yes, he decided, it was time. Time to bring Lucas

in and show him, and watch his face as he understood who held the whip hand. Tonight would be good.

He reached for the phone.

'No, don't *touch* me!' Mellie cried, twisting away from his hand.

'Now, Mellie, you're all upset. Calm down a little. After all, you made the deals. What did you expect?'

She had scrunched up against the car door, as far from him as she could get, but she couldn't take her eyes off his face. Once again she felt that eerie sense of unreality, the same as at the breakfast table a few minutes before. Everything was so peaceful, so perfect. The gentle breeze, the gulls floating overhead, kids laughing and running across the emerald sward of the square. A perfect small town day. And beneath its skin, the black rot of evil.

It was on his face. She could see it now. His expression was perfectly bland, as if he had no idea what she saw, or what he had done.

But she *knew*.

'Lucas, how did Gage's belt get around Larry's neck?'

He shrugged. 'Gage put it there, I reckon. How else?'

'Did you give it back to Gage, then?'

His eyelids flickered. 'Give it back? What are you talking about, girl?'

'I saw you!' she burst out, frantic. 'I saw you pick it up, that night, down by the river. *You* had that belt, not Gage. So how did it get around Larry's neck?'

He sighed and leaned back. 'So that's it.' He shook his head. 'Mellie, Mellie. I don't know what you think you saw that night, but you'd just been raped. You weren't in any condition to see anything. Probably hallucinating, if it comes to it.'

But he wasn't denying it, he was only denying her. And her certainty grew.

'I won't let you do it,' she said.

'Mellie, you just relax.' He reached for her, and she screamed.

'No, don't *touch* me!' The thought of his hands on her made her want to vomit. What kind of devil was he? He'd killed Larry to take care of Gage. And he wanted her to be a part of that? That it was the result of some unholy deal he thought she'd made?

'I won't,' she said again. 'I'll go to the police. I'll tell them everything. Gage didn't do it. You did.'

For a long moment, then, silence. A car went past, its radio playing a Rolling Stones tune: 'Sympathy for the Devil'.

And as she watched his face, the hidden thing beneath his skin reared up and looked out of his

233

eyes, laughing at her. Just for a moment, but it was enough.

'Fuck your deals, Lucas. I'm not any part of them.'

'Two deals, Mellie,' he said. 'You remember, don't you? Larry gave you to me, to save his hide, and you said yes. You can't have forgotten. And then I told you Gage wouldn't worry you any more, and you agreed to that, too. Free will, Mellie. Your own choice. And now you want to back out?'

'Take me to the jail, Lucas. I'm done with talking to you.'

He shook his head. 'I'm not taking you anywhere, Mellie. You'll just make a fool of yourself. What have you got to say? That you think you saw something, in the dark, just after you got raped by Gage Temple? Who's going to put any stock in that?'

His words beat on her like a hard rain, but she was past caring. All she wanted was to get away from him, to run down these soft and pleasant and corrupt streets, shouting the truth about him, about Trinity, at the top of her lungs. Her right hand shot out and yanked at the door handle. And nothing happened.

'Mellie.'

His voice was so cold it froze the marrow of her bones. She'd always wondered about that expression, and now she understood. It was as if her skin was freezing from the inside out, as if that awful feeling you get in your chest when you eat ice cream too fast had spread and filled up her body. She waited, clenched in upon herself until finally a shred of warmth returned to her.

Slowly, she turned back to face him, and gasped at what she saw on his face. Something swollen, bloated, ancient. Like a stone slimed by some prehistoric mould – hard, pitiless, knowing.

'I take it you don't intend to keep our deals, is that it?'

'I told you,' she whispered weakly. 'We ain't got no deals, and we never did have.'

'Oh, yes we did. But what the hell. I'm a sport, Mellie. I'll let you out of them. Both of them, one, and two. Just like that, what do you think?'

His words dropped like hot stones into the cacophony of her confused thoughts, and for a moment she understood what was wrong with those words. Acknowledging them would admit they were real, would admit that, even as she now renounced them, at one time she had recognized his unholy pacts.

But in her extremity she pushed these thoughts away, and grasped at the spurious release he seemed to offer. 'No deals, Lucas. Never were no deals.'

But he only grinned – her skin crawled at that, she closed her eyes because she could actually feel her flesh moving, as if ants were crawling around *under* her skin – and then he said, 'Third time pays all, Mellie. One more deal. And this time it *is* a deal. You want Gage out of this, free as a bird? I can do it. But you pay for it, you understand? No getting around it, you make your *deal*, and you make it with *me!*'

She had wadded her right fist up against her mouth, and now she tasted blood from the pressure of it as she stared at him. Everything she'd ever feared was somehow wrapped up in his words – their portent was awful, and she knew if she agreed to them, her payment would be more than she could bear.

But could she let an innocent man die? Gage hadn't killed those boys. This monster across from her had done that. And she'd never been more sure of anything in her life. Gage was a brutal, cruel man, but he didn't deserve this.

So why did she also detect, beneath the rind of Lucas and his tricky promises, a sadness so deep it made her want to scream?

'What do you want?' she said at last; knowing even as she spoke, that her last lifeline was slipping through her fingers forever.

He was silent for a long moment, and once again, as she looked into his eyes, she felt that hint of sadness so sharp and pure it was almost inhuman. Then he blinked, and it was gone. His next words were slow, clear, and perfectly without inflection.

'If you want to save Gage Temple, Mellie,

then you are going to have to keep him.'

She didn't understand at first, but then he told her, and the horror of it came clear when he took out the small, velvet lined box and gave it to her . . .

Just before they pulled away from the curb, he said, 'Oh, and one final thing, Mellie. You owe me something for this, and I will collect it one day. You owe me a birth, a son. I will come for that when I'm ready. You're family, now, Mellie, and that's all there is to it. Do you agree?'

Utterly spent and broken, and feeling as if she had no will of her own left at all, she nodded.

'Say it, Mellie. Say, yes, I understand, Lucas. I owe you a son. It's a deal.'

Her mouth and tongue and lips had no more feeling than if a dentist had put a jackhammer load of Novocaine into her, but she thought on each word as she spoke, and she got it all out. And if one part of her prayed for death, a different part of her knew she wouldn't get it. Not before she kept her side of the bargain.

'Well, good enough, Mellie. I admire you, I guess. To make a sacrifice like this. Hell, some folks would say you're almost a saint. Yes, I believe they would.'

He slapped the shifter into first and glided away from the curb, turning towards the county jail.

'Some folks would,' he said again. 'Not me, though.'

* * *

Sheriff Hank Culpepper had held his office for almost twenty years. Every four years, like clockwork, he ran for re-election, though each time after the first, the outcome was always a foregone conclusion. In Fulton County, elections were mostly formalities. What really mattered was what a few men, particularly Preacher Christopher Buck, wanted to happen. And for two decades, those men had been quite happy with Hank Culpepper, and things had been good because of that.

He thought on this as he pushed his office chair back from his desk. If it had been anybody else but the young man seated across from him, smiling that damned smile, he wouldn't have paid one whit of attention to the story he'd just heard.

Back in the cells Gage Temple was still snoozing away, and when he woke up, the Sheriff intended to let him know he had him dead bang on a first degree murder charge. And maybe more than one. He'd been smiling about that all morning, because the physical evidence tied a whole bunch of problems up in one neat package.

And now here was Lucas Buck and a sixteen-year-old piece of white trash blowing it all to bits. But it *was* Lucas Buck, whose daddy was Preacher Christopher Buck, and over the last twenty years, Sheriff Culpepper had learned that attention must be paid.

He didn't like it, though.

'Let's go through that one more time?' he said.

'Sure, Sheriff. It's easy. You got old Gage Temple locked up for murdering Larry Rosenweig, but he didn't do it.' Lucas spread his hands and grinned, as if what he'd just said was the simplest thing in the world.

'And he didn't do it because . . . ?' Sheriff Culpepper prompted.

'Because he was with Melanie Hankings, here, when he was supposed to be out murdering Larry.'

'Uh huh.' The Sheriff probed for an irritating bit of his late luncheon burger that had gotten caught in a broken filling. He glanced brightly at Mellie. 'That what you say, girl?'

Mellie felt as if her head had turned into a balloon. The sound of her own voice echoed thinly in that emptiness. 'Yes, Sheriff, Gage was with me till late last night. I was with him, rather. We was driving around, talking.'

'Um hm, talking about what, again?'

'Gage asked me to marry him. He gave me this ring.' And once again, she offered the small velvet box.

'So you and him are engaged?'

'That's right, Sheriff. You can check down at the Rice Jewelry, Gage bought me this. He'd been fixing to surprise me, though I guess a lot of folks knew about it already.'

The Sheriff rubbed his chin. 'OK. So if Gage didn't do it, how did it get done? What about his belt?'

'Like I said, Sheriff,' Lucas continued, 'Gage and me had a fight down by the river a while back. He tried to whip on me with that belt of his. You know how he keeps it all sharpened up.'

The Sheriff nodded. He did know. His boys had fished enough men out of the Country House Pub with the marks of Gage's belt on their hides.

'Go on,' he said.

'Well,' Lucas shrugged and grinned, 'I just took it away from that old boy and threw it in the brush. Gave her a real good toss, cause I didn't want him getting his hands on it again. Then I kicked in his ribs. You know his ribs are all broken up. Well, that was me. That's how it happened, you can ask him.'

'So anybody could have found that belt?'

'I guess somebody did, Sheriff. And I already told you who I think it was.'

'Yep. Why don't you tell me again?'

'Marvis Pickney come to me with a burlap bag. There was what I told you in that bag, and a note. I don't know how Larry Rosenweig found out about Earl and his boys, but he must have. And he was purely crazy to think he could have it out with those stump jumpers all by himself, but I guess he did. He wrote them a note calling them out, and it got him killed, looks like.

'One of them Pickney brats must have found the

belt, and old Earl was just smart enough to think it would be a good way to put the blame for what he did onto somebody else. Onto Gage.'

The Sheriff nodded. 'And you got that bag and that note over to your place. So how come Marvis gave it to you?'

'I don't know for sure, Sheriff. He said he hadn't opened it, but Earl had told him to get rid of it. And he worried, 'cause he was afraid he was mixing into something too deep for him. So he brought it to me. That's what he said, at least.'

'You and Marvis are real good friends, is that it?'

'I hardly know Marvis at all. Bought a little shine from him every once in a while. Maybe I was just the most respectable person he knew he thought he could trust.'

Sheriff Culpepper wished he hadn't spoken to the radio station reporter as quick as he had. This whole story seemed to him as thin as well water, but it put a whole spanner wrench into his plans. And the wrench seemed to be coming from the Buck family, which was nothing at all to ignore.

'You tell your daddy about this . . . story?'

'My daddy don't have anything to do with it, Sheriff. It's the truth, is all.'

Which was something Sheriff Culpepper had more than a few doubts about. But Lucas had sewed it up neatly. If he was right, Gage had a witness and an alibi. And there was the ring in that girl's hand for proof.

He thought some more on it. He didn't really give a fuck who got fried for the crimes, as long as somebody did. And Earl Pickney would make as good a barbecue as anybody, if that's what Lucas and his daddy wanted.

He couldn't figure out *why* they wanted it, but this wouldn't be the first time he'd gone along. He just wanted to be sure.

'Lucas,' he said at last. 'Are you positive this is the way things went?'

Lucas leaned forward and stared straight into his eyes. 'Sure, Sheriff, it's exactly how it happened. What else could it be?'

They stared at each other for a long, long moment, and at the end, the Sheriff dropped his eyes. 'OK,' he said. 'That's the way it is, then. I'll be sending one of my deputies with you to pick up that bag, if it's OK with you.'

Lucas nodded. 'Fine with me. One thing, though. Let me be the one to tell old Gage. He ought to be awake by now.'

As it turned out, he was.

Gage woke up with his head ringing like a cracked church bell. His ribs felt as if somebody had kicked them in all over again. Everything seemed to have a yellow haze over it. He blinked, and waited for things to come into focus. After a while they did, and he saw the bars surrounding him on all sides.

And he saw Lucas Buck leaning over him, smiling.

'What . . . ?' he mumbled.

Lucas spoke softly and clearly. Each word somehow hammered through Gage's jaundiced fog and nailed itself deep into his throbbing brain.

'They have you for the murder of Larry Rosenweig and probably for that negro boy, Gage, and they are going to fry your worthless ass into butter,' Lucas said. 'Unless you do exactly what I say. We got a deal, Gage?'

Gage stared around blankly. Not one bit of it made any sense, but he believed anyway. He couldn't help it. Something about Lucas Buck in that moment was utterly irresistible, and he knew that his life was hanging in the balance. A terror as deep as anything he'd ever felt in his whole life swept over him in a sudden, overwhelming flood. He felt his bladder begin to go, and he clenched himself.

'Deal,' he whispered, with the same reflex that compels a drowning man to shout for help, or a man falling off a cliff to scream.

'Good. First thing, right now you give me that note in your pocket. Second thing, where is Marvis likely to be?'

Shuddering, Gage gave him the note. Then he told him, as well as he could guess, where to find Marvis.

'That's real good, Gage. Now if anybody asks, all you remember was you were celebrating. Got

243

that? Celebrating. You weren't anywhere near the river last night, you were celebrating. Got that?'

Through lips that felt like spoiled liver, Gage managed to mumble, 'Sure, Lucas. Celebrating what?'

'Why, boy, your engagement to Mellie Hankings. Don't tell me you forgot.'

Dumb as a stretch of asphalt, Gage stared up at him.

'And let me be the first to congratulate you,' Lucas said. 'I'm sure the two of you will be very happy.'

Chapter Thirteen

'What's Marie look so happy about, Daddy?' Lucas asked, as he stuck a fork into a tall wedge of her homemade carrot cake.

The Preacher adjusted the snowy white napkin he'd tucked into his collar, and eyed his own piece of cake with satisfaction. 'Well, boy, what do you think? I mean, her being what you might call one of my fans, and all.'

Lucas grinned. 'Fans, Daddy? Is that anything like those groupies the rock and roll bands have?'

The Preacher's cheeks suddenly flushed pink. He knew what groupies were for. But how could Lucas know anything like that about him and Marie?

'How's your cake?' he said finally.

'It's just fine, Daddy. Are we about ready to quit dancing now?'

'What are you talking about?'

Lucas shrugged. 'I thought we weren't supposed to *be* talking much anymore. You know, ever since you kind of threw me out of the family?'

Marie bustled in, still grinning like a raccoon, and began to clear the rest of the dishes. Both men waited till she had retreated back into the kitchen. Then the Preacher said, 'Well, I guess we could discuss that, Lucas.'

'Isn't anything to discuss, Daddy,' Lucas replied.

'Oh, isn't there? How you been doing lately? Everything OK?'

Lucas shrugged. 'Fine as paint, Daddy.'

'Thought you might have been against me on that Vietnam memorial thing. Now that didn't turn out so well, did it?'

Lucas finished cleaning his plate and pushed it away. He leaned back in his chair and stretched. 'Damnedest thing about that, wasn't it? Those crazy Pickneys. Been too many brothers jumping too many sisters back in the woods, seems like. You ever hear of anything so dumb?'

The Preacher nodded slowly. 'Uh huh. I guess so. You know, I talked to the Sheriff about that. He thought he had old Gage for it, you know.'

'But he was wrong, wasn't he?'

The Preacher lifted his napkin from his collar, folded it carefully, and placed it beside his plate. 'You know, he asked me about that, too. Whether I thought he was wrong. You know what I said?'

'Yes, I do,' Lucas replied. 'You told him I had the right of it, and to hang Earl Pickney from the highest tree he could find.'

The Preacher started. 'Now how did you know that?'

'A little bird, Daddy. Anyway, it is the truth.'

'Well, hell, Lucas. What's the truth, anyway?'

'You got that right,' Lucas told him. 'Here in Trinity, anyway.'

They sat in silence then, each with their own thoughts. On the Preacher's face was an expression of triumph. Lucas merely looked distant and thoughtful. Finally, he shifted. 'You want to get to it, then?'

The Preacher pushed back his chair and stood up. 'Might as well,' he said.

Lucas nodded. 'Isn't any need to stand up, Daddy. We aren't going anywhere.'

The Preacher paused. 'Lucas, I'm just trying to make it easy on you. You know what you have to do. It's in the blood.'

'I already told you, Daddy. I'm not submitting to anything, not on this earth, and not in hell, either.'

A vein began to throb in the Preacher's forehead. He swung around slowly and stared at Lucas as if he'd just discovered him sitting there.

'Is that so?' he said at last. 'Well, then, may I ask just what in the hell you came over here for?'

Lucas grinned. 'Why sure, Daddy. Ask away.'

'Don't play with me, boy.'

'Oh, I'm not. I guess you figured to drag me back out to your freak show down in the graveyard, and

247

beat on me some more? Submit, boy, submit, and all that?'

Preacher Buck's head suddenly looked as if it were swelling. His neck bulged over the top of his collar, and his skin began to turn thick and red.

'You're mocking me, boy? Aren't you? And mocking the blood, and the family? By *God*—'

'God, Daddy? I don't know God has anything to do with it. Just the opposite, I'd say.'

The Preacher whirled and slammed his meaty fist down on the table. China and cutlery jumped. 'Not another word, boy. Not one more damned word, you hear me?'

'Oh, I hear you, Daddy. I guess you want me to go now?'

The Preacher said nothing.

'OK, then, I guess we're done here,' Lucas said, rising from his chair. 'Oh, by the way, one more thing. About that graveyard of yours.'

It took the Preacher an effort to get it out, but he did. He didn't notice he was grinding his teeth. 'What's that?'

'Well, we won't have to worry about it anymore. Seeing as it won't be with us much longer.' Lucas grinned and turned for the door. 'Night, now, Daddy. You take care.'

'Wait!'

'Hm? What's that, Daddy?'

'What do you think you're talking about?'

Lucas stopped. 'I guess you haven't heard, then.

Some company from up in Wilmington, I think it's called the Renaissance Group, it bought the mortgage on that land from Orville Willis down at the Merchants. Rumour is, they plan to put up one of those little shopping malls? Good thing, too. That land is prime, and it's just going to waste out there.'

Small puffing sounds began to issue from the Preacher's mouth. He didn't seem to notice them, either, but Lucas couldn't help grinning. His father looked like a big tea kettle about to boil over.

'You lost your mind, boy? You can't do that.'

'Me? I'm not doing anything, Daddy.'

'You think I don't know what the fuck the Renaissance Group is, Lucas? You think I'm a fool? I'll have Orville Willis's balls for cat food over this, see if I don't. He must have lost his mind, too.'

But Lucas shook his head. 'Oh, I don't think you got the weight for that. Not down at the Merchants, anyway. See, this Renaissance Group evidently owns the lion's share over there. Orville knows which side his bread is buttered on.'

Now the colour drained from the Preacher's face as if his blood had been poured down his neck. 'I— you can't. They can't just foreclose. I'll pay the damned thing off!'

'With what, Daddy? I hear you don't have any ready cash. Nothing you can get to in time, that is. Too bad about that, but . . . what the hell.' He shrugged. 'I'll kind of miss that old swamp, but you know what they say. How the cookie crumbles and everything.'

He paused, then raised one finger. 'Tell you what I'll do, though. I'll make sure they get Mama's bones moved back to the big graveyard, before the bulldozers come in.'

Slowly, as if he were a balloon leaking air, the Preacher subsided. He groped for the back of his chair, found it, and lowered himself into it. 'Lucas . . .'

'What, Daddy?'

'I . . . you win.'

'Win what, Daddy? Are we playing for something?'

The Preacher put his hands over his face. 'Lucas, don't do this. Don't make me do this. I . . . I'm not ready yet. Please, son . . . I'm not ready.'

And now Lucas came to him, and lightly placed his fingers on the old man's shoulders. 'Oh, don't worry, Daddy. It won't be as bad as you think. Not like the old ways. I told you, I'm not dancing to any tune, not of blood or family. It'll be OK. You'll see.'

But then he stopped and stepped back, an expression of fearful splendour shining suddenly from his face. 'Say it, Daddy.'

'I— no . . .'

'Say it!'

Deep inside himself, the Preacher could see it now. A great spinning ball of black fire. It had warmed him all his life, filled his veins with ten generations of blood, and his muscles with unearthly strength. But now that light was fading, receding even as he reached for it.

Going, going . . . gone.

'I submit,' he whispered. 'Don't do it, Lucas. I submit.'

Lucas slapped him hard on the back. It knocked him forward a bit, and so, blessedly, he couldn't see what was in Lucas's eyes.

'Then we got us a deal, Daddy.'

'Lucas . . .'

'Go on, say the rest. You know I have to hear it.' And, oddly enough, what sounded beneath Lucas's words was entirely unexpected. It was kindness.

The Preacher nodded.

'Deal, Lucas.'

Lucas nodded. 'Come on, Daddy. Let me help you up. We're done here, I think.'

And with that the Preacher stood. He looked like an old man now, dazed and confused. He leaned on Lucas's arm as they shambled towards the door.

'Where we going, boy?'

'Back to the big house, Daddy. I'm taking you home. You belong to me now, but don't you worry. I'll take real good care of you.'

As it all slid away from him, the Preacher could only think that it had happened so easily, and it didn't hurt nearly as much as he'd thought it would. In a way, it was almost a relief, to lay it down. Lay down the burden of the blood.

To rest in the everlasting bosom of the – what was the word? Everything was fading so fast. He spoke the word aloud, almost without realizing it.

'Family?' he whispered.

'That's right, Daddy,' Lucas said soothingly. 'Family.'

As Lucas spoke the word, out beyond the orchard, across the bobwire fence, beneath the light of the always bloated moon, the stones flared in one burst of rotten, putrescent light, as if acknowledging, for the first time in their dreadful existence, a master.

Lucas smiled.

'Come on, Daddy. Let's go home.'

THE END

THE EXORCIST
by William Peter Blatty

The most famous novel of satanism and possession ever written.

The terror began unobtrusively. Noises in Regan's room, an odd smell, misplaced furniture, an icy chill. Easy explanations are offered. Then changes begin to show in eleven-year-old Regan – severe and frightening. Medical tests shed no light on her symptoms, but it is as if a different personality has invaded the child.

Father Damien Karras, a Jesuit priest, is called in. Is it possible that a demonic force is at large? Might exorcism be the answer?

Made into a terrifying film, *The Exorcist* has sold over twelve million copies, and is a landmark in the history of popular literature.

0 552 09156 1

A SICKNESS OF THE SOUL
by Simon Maginn

'It was a bigger story than I'd imagined, and at the centre of it was Teacher. I was determined now, more than ever, to get the story, the whole story. I would do whatever was necessary.'

When Robert, an investigative journalist, tunes into a phone-in programme while driving through the Midlands, he immediately realizes he is on to something. He goes undercover to infiltrate a bizarre bikers' cult, the Sons of the New Bethlehem, led by the charismatic Teacher. It is Teacher whom Robert has heard on the radio, giving advice to distraught callers and praying for their salvation. Teacher's ministry is a fully-fledged crusade, in leather. Astride their Harleys and Hondas, the gang – Spider, Loverman, Stroker, Biceps and the rest – gather in shopping centres and car parks with the aim of winning converts for Christ.

Robert's cover, however, is not as good as he'd thought, and he finds himself prisoner of the Sons, cooped up in an eerie hotel. Trying to penetrate the enigmatic facade of Teacher, and to discover what, *exactly*, is the man's method of healing his followers, he becomes involved in a series of deaths before he can escape. And when he's back in London with his partner, Fiona, he can't settle into his former life. The memories of Teacher's weird regime haunt him, and before long he's on the road to the Midlands once more . . .

0 552 14250 6

MARY REILLY
Valerie Martin

'GRIPPING . . . IT HAS A COMPLEXITY THAT EXCITES
THE MIND AND A BEAUTIFUL SIMPLICITY THAT
KNOTS THE HEART'
Isabel Quigly, *Financial Times*

Mary Reilly is a young Victorian housemaid in
the employ of an elderly bachelor. When her
master asks her about the strange scars on her
hands and neck, she reveals that she was
tortured as a child by her alcoholic father. This
revelation is the beginning of regular
conversations between master and servant,
conversations which she records each night in
the journal she keeps in her attic room.

Strange things begin to happen in the
household. Her master is often ill or locked
away in his laboratory for days on end. Who is
the strange and sinister young man he employs,
and why is her master, a kindly doctor well
known for his intelligence and philanthropy, so
involved with him?

As the tension mounts, Mary learns that things
are not always as they appear and, to her horror,
begins to understand the dark and terrible secret
of her employer . . .

'*MARY REILLY* IS AN ASTONISHING *TOUR DE FORCE*'
Margaret Atwood

0 552 99391 3

BLACK SWAN

A SELECTED LIST OF FINE TITLES
AVAILABLE FROM CORGI AND
BLACK SWAN

THE PRICES SHOWN BELOW WERE CORRECT AT THE TIME OF GOING TO PRESS.
HOWEVER TRANSWORLD PUBLISHERS RESERVE THE RIGHT TO SHOW NEW
RETAIL PRICES ON COVERS WHICH MAY DIFFER FROM THOSE PREVIOUSLY
ADVERTISED IN THE TEXT OR ELSEWHERE.

99588 6	THE HOUSE OF THE SPIRITS	Isabel Allende	£6.99
99618 1	BEHIND THE SCENES AT THE MUSEUM	Kate Atkinson	£6.99
09156 1	THE EXORCIST	William Peter Blatty	£4.99
99632 7	NATALYA, GOD'S MESSENGER	Magda Bogin	£5.99
99531 2	AFTER THE HOLE	Guy Burt	£5.99
99532 0	SOPHIE	Guy Burt	£5.99
99602 5	THE LAST GIRL	Penelope Evans	£5.99
14043 0	SHADOW PLAY	Frances Fyfield	£4.99
14223 9	BORROWED TIME	Robert Goddard	£5.99
13840 1	CLOSED CIRCLE	Robert Goddard	£5.99
99616 5	SIMPLE PRAYERS	Michael Golding	£5.99
99656 4	THE TEN O'CLOCK HORSES	Laurie Graham	£5.99
99169 4	GOD KNOWS	Joseph Heller	£7.99
99567 3	SAILOR SONG	Ken Kesey	£6.99
14111 9	HOUSE OF TRIBES	Gary Kilworth	£4.99
99542 8	SWEET THAMES	Matthew Kneale	£6.99
14249 2	VIRGINS AND MARTYRS	Simon Maginn	£4.99
14250 6	A SICKNESS OF THE SOUL	Simon Maginn	£4.99
99391 3	MARY REILLY	Valerie Martin	£6.99
99392 1	THE GREAT DIVORCE	Valerie Martin	£6.99
99502 9	THE LAST WORD	Paul Micou	£5.99
99596 7	BLOODSUCKING FIENDS	Christopher Moore	£6.99
99709 9	THEORY OF MIND	Sanjida O'Connell	£6.99
99667 X	GHOSTING	John Preston	£6.99
99664 5	YELLOWHEART	Tracy Reed	£5.99
99696 3	THE VISITATION	Sue Reidy	£5.99
99636 X	KNOWLEDGE OF ANGELS	Jill Paton Walsh	£5.99
99673 4	DINA'S BOOK	Herbjørg Wassmo	£6.99

All Transworld titles are available by post from:

Book Service By Post, PO Box 29, Douglas, Isle of Man IM99 1BQ

Credit cards accepted. Please telephone 01624 675137, fax 01624
670923 or Internet http://www. bookpost.co.uk for details.

Please allow £0.75 per book for post and packing UK.
Overseas customers allow £1 per book for post and packing.